MW01077329

For Megan and Iris, two spectacular girls whose humour, tenacity and zest for life amaze me every single day. Love you, girls. – L.B.

For my mum Janet, my sister Hannah, and my daughter Maisie. Three generations of spectacular women. Xxx – E.M.

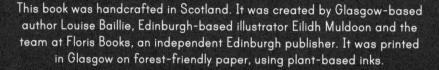

This book belongs to

This book was handcrafted in Scotland. It was created by Glasgow-based author Louise Baillie, Edinburgh-based illustrator Eilidh Muldoon and the team at Floris Books, an independent Edinburgh publisher. It was printed in Glasgow on forest-friendly paper, using plant-based inks.

FSC
www.fsc.org
MIX
Paper | Supporting
responsible forestry
FSC® C007785

First published by Floris Books in 2023. Text © 2023 Louise Baillie. Illustrations © 2023 Eilidh Muldoon. Louise Baillie and Eilidh Muldoon have asserted their right under the Copyright, Designs and Patent Act 1988 to be identified as the Author and Illustrator of this Work. All rights reserved. No part of this book may be reproduced without the prior permission of Floris Books, Edinburgh www.florisbooks.co.uk British Library CIP Data available ISBN 978-178250-864-9 Printed in Great Britain by Bell & Bain Ltd

SPECTACULAR SCOTTISH WOMEN

Celebrating inspiring lives from Scotland

Written by
LOUISE BAILLIE

Illustrated by
EILIDH MULDOON

Kelpies World

MEET SCOTLAND'S SPECTACULAR WOMEN!

10 Annie Lennox

14 Victoria Drummond

18 Rose Reilly

22 Jackie Kay

26 Mary, Queen of Scots

30 Evelyn Glennie

34 Corinne Hutton

38 Sophia Jex-Blake

42 Emeli Sandé

46 Karen Gillan

50 Mary Somerville

54 Lorraine Kelly

58 Jeannie Robertson

62 Liz McColgan

66 Joan Eardley

70 Roza Salih

74 Elsie Inglis

78 Catherine Heymans

82 Mary Barbour

86 Anne Lorne Gillies

90 Flora MacDonald

94 Ali Smith

98 Eunice Olumide

102 Jennie Lee

106 Kayleigh Haggo

110 Jane Haining

114 Iona Fyfe

118 Nosheena Mobarik

122 Jessie Valentine

126 Laura Young

Welcome to *Spectacular Scottish Women*!

Scotland is home to countless strong, creative and inspiring women, from authors to athletes, scientists to singers, and actors to activists! I wrote this book because I wanted to celebrate their awesome achievements and tell the world their stories — so many of them are not well known.

These spectacular women have different backgrounds and talents, but they were all born in Scotland or chose to make Scotland their home. This country is so much richer for their work and efforts. It has been a joy to find out more about them, and to see them come to life on these pages thanks to talented illustrator Eilidh Muldoon.

When I was working on this book, as well as reading about the women's lives, it felt important to me to speak to them personally if possible. They told me their stories and now you can hear their voices too.

Thank you to Anne, Catherine, Corinne, Emeli, Eunice, Evelyn, Iona, Kayleigh, Laura, Liz, Lorraine, Nosheena, Rose and Roza. Thank you also to Mrs Annette Lantos and her daughter Katherine, who talked so movingly about Jane; to Susan Stewart, an expert on Jennie; and to Eve Soulsby, who patiently answered my questions and shared her book about Jessie.

Thank you to my readers too: I hope these spectacular Scottish women will inspire you to follow in their footsteps and achieve all your ambitions. Go and make your mark on the world, just like they did!

Louise Baillie
Glasgow

ANNIE LENNOX

Singer, Musician and Activist

Born Aberdeen, 1954

When Annie left home to study flute and piano at the Royal Academy of Music in London, it was just the start of her incredible musical journey. The shy Aberdeen teenager would go on to become one of music's most iconic stars.

She sang in a couple of pop bands while studying, but when she formed Eurythmics alongside Dave Stewart in 1980 she really made an impact. Annie didn't believe that women and girls had to have long hair or wear skirts. She cropped her hair, dyed it orange and wore men's clothes, challenging ideas about how women should dress and inspiring fans all over the world.

Eurythmics' sound was unique too: their use of big beats, electronic synthesisers and Annie's soulful, powerful voice made global hits. They sold 75 million records worldwide and were one of the most successful bands of the 1980s.

DRESSED FOR SUCCESS

Annie wore both men's and women's clothes in famous music videos, like Eurythmics' 'Love Is a Stranger' and 'Sweet Dreams (Are Made of This)'. She says, "I love to be an individual, to step beyond gender."

"I want to utilise whatever voice I have towards empowerment, towards inspiration, towards justice."

In 1992 Annie launched a hugely successful solo career, recording even more hits and receiving both praise and prizes.

AWARD-WINNING ANNIE

Annie has won many awards for her solo career. She won Best British Female at the Brit Awards a record six times, as well as four Grammy Awards and a Golden Globe for Best Original Song with 'Into the West' from the film soundtrack of *The Lord of the Rings: The Return of the King*.

Annie realised her success meant people would listen to her, and decided to use her voice to support those in need: "I'm a mother, I'm a woman, I'm a human being, I'm an artist and hopefully I'm an advocate." After visiting South Africa in 2003 and seeing the misery caused by HIV and AIDS, she decided to help. Annie persuaded 23 famous singers, including superstars like Madonna, Pink and Celine Dion, to join her in recording a song called 'Sing', which raised money and awareness to help stop the spread of HIV, and support women and girls living with it. She strongly believes that music has the power to change lives: "A song has the potential to make a person react: to choke up, to want to cry or to want to dance. It's that response that gets me, and everyone can access that."

"I'm a mother, I'm a woman, I'm a human being, I'm an artist and hopefully I'm an advocate."

SCOTTISH SOUL

Annie has been acclaimed as one of the greatest white soul singers ever and teamed up with American soul legend Al Green on 'Put a Little Love in Your Heart', and Stevie Wonder, who played harmonica on Eurythmics' 1985 No. 1 single 'There Must Be an Angel (Playing with My Heart)'. Annie also duetted with Queen of Soul Aretha Franklin on feminist anthem 'Sisters Are Doin' It for Themselves'.

Annie has also worked with charities and organisations like Comic Relief, Oxfam, Greenpeace and Amnesty International. She has not only used her voice on No. 1 songs, she has raised her voice to make a difference in the world.

EMPOWERING GIRLS WORLDWIDE

In 2008, Annie founded a charity called The Circle, which helps women and girls. It supports women's refuges, raises awareness of women's legal rights, and works against the kinds of poverty and violence that particularly affect women and girls.

VICTORIA DRUMMOND

Marine Engineer

Born Errol, Perthshire, 1894

Victoria was born into a wealthy family at the end of the nineteenth century. She grew up at Megginch Castle in Perthshire, yet her interests were very different from those expected of young ladies: she was fascinated by machinery and finding out how things worked.

She visited engineering works close to her home and told the owner she wanted to be a marine engineer, working on ships and sailing around the world. Unusually for the early 1900s, her family encouraged her ambition. Aged 21, Victoria completed an apprenticeship at the Northern Garage in Perth while studying maths and engineering at night classes. After gaining more experience with a company in Dundee, at age 25 she became the first female marine engineer in the UK.

QUEENLY GODMOTHER

Victoria was named after family friend Queen Victoria, who was also her godmother.

Victoria's first job was on a passenger liner called *Anchises*, sailing to Australia and China. Although her work was excellent, she faced sexist comments from some passengers and crew, who couldn't accept a woman being an engineer.

During the Second World War, Victoria worked both at sea and on land. She was an air-raid warden in London and set up a canteen to feed families who had been bombed out of their homes.

PIONEER ENGINEER

In 1920, Victoria became the first female member of the Institute of Marine Engineers. She was inducted into the Scottish Engineering Hall of Fame in 2018.

She also served on several Merchant Navy ships during wartime. In 1940, the SS *Bonita* came under fire from the German airforce when Victoria was in the engine room. She was covered in oil but stayed at her post, sending her colleagues away for their safety. Alone, she repaired the damage and kept the engines working. She wrote in her diary: 'Three great explosions on the port side when bombs fell. One oil box failed from the main engine. Eight lots of great explosions and machine-gun fire all round. Made temporary repairs.' Thanks to Victoria's courage and skill, the ship was saved. She was awarded an MBE and was the first woman to be honoured with a Lloyd's War Medal for Bravery at Sea.

Alone, she repaired the damage and kept the engines working.

After the war, Victoria returned to Scotland and continued to work in shipyards and on boats. She made 49 ocean-going voyages in a 40-year-long career and proved that women could succeed in a traditionally male-dominated profession.

GLOBAL VOYAGER

Victoria sailed all over the world – very few British women would have visited so many different places at this time. Her destinations included: the USA, Canada, South Africa, Kenya, Sierra Leone, India, Sri Lanka, Lebanon, Australia, France and Gibraltar.

UNFAIR FAIL

Victoria was desperate to become a chief engineer, but when she sat the exam, the UK's Board of Trade said she had failed. She took it again, and got the same result. Victoria believed her answers were correct and that she had been failed because she was a woman. She took the exam 37 times! Eventually she was able to sit it while she was outside the UK, in Panama, and she passed first time.

ROSE REILLY

Footballer

Born Kilmarnock, 1955

When Rose was three, she disappeared from her house in Stewarton, Ayrshire, and her mum found her on the nearby football pitch. When she was five, she asked for a ball for Christmas, but got a doll. She swapped the doll for a ball – and slept with it instead! "I slept with my ball for two reasons," Rose explains. "First, because I loved it, and second, I was afraid my mum would take it off me. People thought I was weird, because wee girls didn't play football."

Rose's mum didn't take her ball, but there were plenty of other people at the time who disapproved. Rose says, "I got the belt at school every day for playing football with the boys. I got abuse shouted at me in the street." The local boys' team only let her join if she cut her hair short and pretended her name was Ross. She was their best player, and Celtic FC wanted to sign her – but couldn't when they found out she was a girl.

Yet Rose never gave up. There were a few amateur teams for women, so she became a striker for Stewarton Thistle and won the Scottish Cup before moving to Glasgow team Westthorn United. She even played for Scotland against England. But Rose wanted to be a professional, which means being paid to play at the highest level. For that she had to look beyond her home country. In 1972 she had a trial for Reims, which was one of the first women's teams in France and helped make women's football popular there. She played a match and was signed at half-time, aged 17.

Before long, Rose moved to AC Milan, one of Italy's biggest women's clubs. In contrast to Scotland, Italy supported the growth of women's football. Leagues and teams were well organised and well funded. Rose had been an amateur in Scotland, semi-professional in France, and now, in Italy, she was finally a professional footballer.

But the Scottish Football Association (SFA) was furious, and banned Rose playing in or for Scotland *sine die* – Latin for 'without limit of time'. The SFA gave no official reason for the ban, but many believed they were angry Rose had criticised them and found a way to play elsewhere. Rose says, "I never wasted energy getting annoyed at the SFA – I just kept looking forward."

The pinnacle of her career was winning the 1984 World Cup.

And Rose had plenty to look forward to. Over twenty years, she played for ten Italian sides, winning eight titles in Serie A (the top Italian league), four Italian cups and two Serie A Golden Boots for top goalscorer. The Italian Federation even asked her to play for the Italian national team.

TO CAP IT ALL OFF

In 2019, before the Scotland women's team played Jamaica at Hampden, First Minister Nicola Sturgeon presented Rose and other women from her 1972 Scotland team with the caps they had never received for representing their country against England. The SFA only started giving women caps – which had long been given to the men's team – in 1998.

ROSE REILLY

The pinnacle of her career was winning the 1984 World Cup. Her adopted Italy beat West Germany 3–1, and Rose even scored in the final. She remembers, "I walked around smiling for a week. I followed my dream, and I lived the dream."

HALL OF FAME

Scotland is finally recognising Rose as a pioneer in women's football. In 2007, she was inducted into the Scottish Sport Hall of Fame and was also the first female player inducted into the Scottish Football Hall of Fame.

FOOTBALL'S FUTURE FEMALE STARS

Rose is passionate about encouraging girls to play, and in 2021 she launched the Rose Reilly Football Centre with Ayrshire College to provide free sessions to girls aged five to twelve. Rose says, "There's no reason girls can't play, but we need the footballing world to open up to wee girls. Coaches at all levels have a responsibility to encourage and support them. I love it when girls realise they can play and be part of a team, and that football isn't just for boys."

JACKIE KAY

Poet, Playwright, Novelist and Makar

Born Edinburgh, 1961

When Jackie was a baby, her parents – a white Scottish mum and Nigerian dad – couldn't look after her. A white Scottish couple called Helen and John adopted Jackie and took her into their lively, cheerful home in Bishopbriggs, just outside Glasgow.

John worked for the Communist Party and Helen was Scottish secretary for the Campaign for Nuclear Disarmament. Young Jackie went on demonstrations and marches, determined to make the world a better place. Unfortunately, a better world often seemed out of reach for Jackie herself. No one else in her home town looked like her, and other pupils at school – even some teachers – made racist comments.

When Jackie was 16, she had a motorbike accident. She hit three cars, fractured her leg and landed outside a graveyard. It took 18 months to learn to walk again. Yet she reflected later that coming so close to death had set her on a new path: writing. "It is almost as if you write to assert that you're alive," she said.

RUNNER TO WRITER

Jackie escaped the school bullies on the running track. She won a Scottish Schoolgirls' Championship title and considered becoming a professional athlete.

"My experience of being adopted, and the love I was given and gave back, has been life-defining. I think what defines us most is love."

At school, Jackie found support from her English teacher, who recognised her talent for writing and arranged for her to meet famous Scottish author Alasdair Gray. Gray told her firmly, "There is no doubt about it at all: you are a writer."

I SPY

Teenage Jackie worked as famous novelist John Le Carré's cleaner. She says, "Being a cleaner is great for being a writer. You're listening to everything. You can be a spy, but nobody thinks you're taking anything in."

Around the same time, Jackie began to understand that she was attracted to other women. She recalls, "I remember being very scared. However, coming out changed my life because it meant I did not have to live a lie."

"It was an amazing thing to become Makar. To go from a kid who was called all these different names to representing your country."

Jackie graduated from Stirling University with a degree in English, and her award-winning first book of poetry, *The Adoption Papers*, was published in 1991. The poems tell the story of an adopted child's search for her identity and were inspired by Jackie's own life.

Jackie went on to write award-winning novels, plays and

children's books, often focusing on identity, race, history and family, and all peppered with humour. She also taught writing at universities, becoming Professor of Creative Writing at Newcastle University, as well as Chancellor of the University of Salford.

From 2016 to 2021, Jackie was appointed as Scotland's national poet: the Makar. She created new work, promoted poetry and encouraged young people to write. She says, "It was an amazing thing to become Makar. To go from a kid who was called all these different names to representing your country. It made me feel that somehow, at last, I belonged."

WALKING THE RED DUST ROAD

One of Jackie's most famous works is *Red Dust Road*, a memoir of her childhood and growing up in 1960s Scotland. In the book she tells the story of realising that her skin was a different colour to her adoptive parents', and she takes the reader on the journey to find her birth parents and her identity. She explains, "I went to Nigeria and found my father's ancestral village and the red dust road which had been there in my imagination ever since I was young. It was quite extraordinary to meet it in real life."

RED DUST ROAD
JACKIE KAY

MARY STUART
(MARY, QUEEN OF SCOTS)
Queen of Scotland 1542–1567
Born Linlithgow Palace, West Lothian, 1542

Mary became queen of Scotland at only six days old, after her father, King James V, died. From then on, her life was full of peril. Because she was queen, many powerful people tried to control her.

Mary's mother sent her to the French royal court when she was five, because King Henry VIII of England invaded Scotland to force Mary to marry his son. As a teenager, Mary married the French king's son, but he died. Eighteen-year-old Mary returned to Scotland to rule.

THE FOUR MARYS

Young Mary had four companions also called Mary: Mary Beaton, Mary Seaton, Mary Livingstone and Mary Fleming. They went to France with her, and returned to Scotland with her too. They were known as the 'Four Marys' and were friends with their queen for many years.

Cheering crowds met Mary at Leith docks. There was great public interest in the young queen, who spoke Scots well, among her other languages. During her first years on the throne, Mary travelled all around the country, meeting her subjects. She often rode her own horse rather than use a carriage, because she was a strong rider and loved outdoor activities. She played golf and tennis and kept falcons as well as her many much-loved dogs.

Mary remarried, to her handsome cousin Lord Darnley, and they had a son, James. Yet Darnley wanted Mary to promise he would be king if she died; she refused. Darnley was angry, and arranged the murder of Mary's secretary and friend, David Rizzio. Shortly afterwards, Darnley himself was killed in an explosion. Some people suspected Mary was involved in his death and public opinion turned against her.

> **"I have earnestly wished for liberty and done my utmost to procure it for myself."**

Her situation worsened when she married her third husband, the Earl of Bothwell. Many Scottish lords disliked him, and they imprisoned Mary in Lochleven Castle, on a small island, and forced her to sign a document saying baby James was now king. Yet Mary boldly escaped the island castle by disguising herself as a maid.

Mary gathered an army, but it was defeated by the rebel lords. She fled to England, hoping her cousin Queen Elizabeth I would help her. But Elizabeth worried that Mary wanted to take over as queen of England, so she kept her cousin prisoner – for 19 years.

PUPPY LOVE

Mary loved dogs. One of her many dogs, Geddon, was found under her skirts when she was executed, keeping her company in her final moments.

Mary longed for freedom and never stopped trying to escape, so she could return to Scotland and rule as its rightful queen. She declared, "I do not deny that I have earnestly wished for liberty and done my utmost to procure it for myself." But Elizabeth became more convinced that Mary was plotting against her. Mary always rejected Elizabeth's accusations. Eventually, Elizabeth gave consent for Mary to be beheaded.

Witnesses said that when Mary stepped forward to be executed, she behaved with great dignity and defiance. She believed the tragic end to her life would give her story great power.

DEFIANT QUEEN

When Mary and Elizabeth I each ruled Scotland and England, there was conflict between two religious groups: Catholics and Protestants. Elizabeth I was Protestant and feared Catholics were trying to overthrow her. This is one reason that she ordered the beheading of Mary, who was Catholic.

Just before Mary was executed, she dropped her black outer clothing to reveal a scarlet dress underneath. Red was the colour of Catholic martyrs – people who died for their faith – so the bright dress was Mary's way of saying that she was being killed unjustly. It was her last act of defiance.

EVELYN GLENNIE

Percussionist

Born Aberdeen, 1965

Evelyn grew up on a farm near Methlick, Aberdeenshire. When family and friends got together, they would sing traditional Scottish songs. Evelyn showed a real flair for music and started piano lessons aged eight.

But soon Evelyn noticed that the wind hurt her ears when she was cycling. Doctors told her the pain was caused by the nerves in her ears deteriorating, and she began to lose her hearing. By the time she was in secondary school, Evelyn was profoundly deaf.

Evelyn describes what it was like using hearing aids: "Yes, I could hear more when it came to speech, but music just became this barrage of sound. It was a very painful experience because it was an overload of noise."

THE BEAT GOES ON

Percussion music comes from instruments that are struck to make a sound. This includes drums, tambourine, xylophones, cymbals, gongs and chimes. Although a piano has keys, it is also considered a percussion instrument because the keys connect to hammers that strike strings.

Yet one day, Evelyn's percussion teacher suggested something that would change her life. Striking a timpani drum, the teacher asked if she could *feel* the vibrations. Evelyn took out her hearing aids and paid attention to the sound travelling through her body. She remembers, "Bit by bit, it allowed me to see my body as a great big ear: this was the resonating chamber that I had to receive sound. It changed everything for me."

Evelyn began to play percussion instruments, and soon her dream was to become the world's first full-time solo percussionist. But the pathway wasn't clear. "The Royal Academy of Music in London didn't accept me at first, partly because they couldn't believe an orchestra would accept a deaf musician," she explains. "But others' negativity did me a favour, because it gave me absolute focus on my goal." Eventually she was accepted to study percussion and piano.

Evelyn has performed all over the globe with top orchestras, conductors and artists.

SOUND EFFECTS

Evelyn uses her whole body to listen to music and performs barefoot so she can feel vibrations through the floor. Different parts of her body register different sounds: she feels low sounds in her feet and legs, and high sounds on her face, neck and chest.

EVELYN GLENNIE

And Evelyn *has* achieved her dream of becoming a world-famous solo percussionist. She has performed all over the globe with top orchestras, conductors and artists, released more than forty albums and won two Grammy awards. She made history when she played the first percussion concerto for the BBC Proms at the Royal Albert Hall, and again leading over 1,000 drummers at the Opening Ceremony of the 2012 Olympics in London.

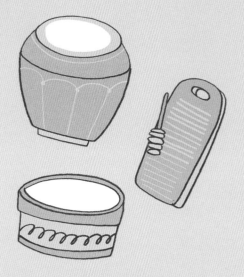

PLAYING FAVOURITES

Evelyn owns over 3,500 percussion instruments, but she can't pick which one she likes best! She says, "They are all my favourites. I made the decision to be a multi-percussion player, therefore whatever is in front of me, that's my favourite."

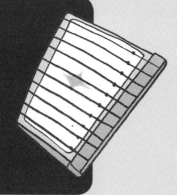

Evelyn believes deafness has made her an exceptional listener: "I have discovered that being a solo percussionist, a career that had not existed before, is all about listening. You are literally listening to yourself and to the audience. I have built my career on listening."

CORINNE HUTTON

Disability Campaigner

Born Bishopbriggs, East Dunbartonshire, 1970

When she was wee, Corinne would climb trees and run around her home town of Lochwinnoch, Renfrewshire. As she grew up she became even more adventurous, walking the Great Wall of China, running the New York Marathon and climbing the Himalayas. Corinne's determination helped her when she became seriously ill aged 43.

Corinne and her family resolved to help other people who had lost limbs.

In 2013, Corinne developed sepsis, an extreme, life-threatening reaction to an infection. Doctors worried she wouldn't survive the night. She received specialist treatment, but a few weeks later, at Glasgow Royal Infirmary, doctors had to amputate her hands and feet because sepsis had damaged them so badly. Corinne remembers, "The focus was on saving my life. I had the most incredible team of people looking after me."

In hospital, Corinne refused to feel sorry for herself and talked to her family about how she could help other people who had lost limbs. She says, "We decided it would be a good idea to set up a charity. I felt I would really have benefitted from speaking to someone who had gone through the same thing."

She launched the charity Finding Your Feet, which visits patients in hospital, organises events, and offers activities such as Pilates and swimming lessons. "It just snowballed!" she says. "We helped people out of isolation in whatever way worked best for them. Soon we had 60 clubs a month running across Scotland."

LIVING THE HIGH LIFE

Corinne still longs for adventure. In 2015 she climbed Scotland's highest mountain, Ben Nevis (1,345m), then moved on to an even bigger challenge in 2018: Kilimanjaro (5,895m) in Tanzania. She was the first female quadruple amputee to do so. "Several times I thought, 'I can't do this,' but I knew I wouldn't give up," Corinne says. "Getting to the top was brilliant."

Corinne used the same pair of prosthetic legs to climb both mountains. "They aren't fancy, they aren't bionic. The fancier your legs are, the more that can go wrong," she explains. "When I climbed Kilimanjaro, I took a pair of boxing gloves and big thick knee pads. If I couldn't wear my legs, it meant I would be able to crawl up. I knew I would resort to that if I needed to."

MOUNT KILIMANJARO

CONGRATULATIONS YOU ARE NOW AT

UHURU PEAK, TANZANIA, 5895M

AFRICA'S HIGHEST POINT

WORLD'S HIGHEST FREESTANDING MOUNTAIN

FUNDRAISING STAR

Corinne's climb up Kilimanjaro raised £30,000 for Finding Your Feet, contributing to the £1.2 million total raised for the charity since 2013.

Corinne made history in January 2019 when she became the first Scot to receive a double hand transplant. She says, "I'm always thinking about my donor's family. They lost someone, and I'll never forget that. I'm so thankful to them."

It might have taken surgeons 14 hours to transplant Corinne's new hands, but she felt them working immediately: "I could wiggle my fingers just after the surgery. They felt like my hands straight away." Corinne has to do hours of physiotherapy exercises every day to keep her new hands working properly, but they have made a huge difference to her life: "I can do things I never thought possible. I can ruffle my son's hair again!"

SURGICAL SKILLS

When Corinne had her double hand transplant, the surgeon who had amputated her hands six years before was part of the team that transplanted her new ones.

SOPHIA JEX-BLAKE

Doctor and Women's Hospital Founder

Born Hastings, England, 1840

When Sophia was a teenager, she was determined not to settle down and get married, as Victorian society expected young women to do. She had been taught at home and at private school, and she wanted to go on to further study – but her parents refused at first.

Eventually she managed to persuade them, and she attended Queen's College in London. While a student, she was offered a job teaching maths at the college. However, teaching was not her dream: she wanted to become a doctor. Sophia lived at a time when only men trained to be doctors. Some people believed women were not clever enough.

But in 1869, aged 29, Sophia applied to the University of Edinburgh to study medicine. She was told the university would not change its policy on accepting female students

SOPHIA IN AMERICA

Before Sophia studied in Edinburgh, she travelled to the USA and worked as an assistant at the New England Hospital for Women and Children. She applied to Harvard in 1867 to study medicine but was rejected because she was female.

"We walked up to the gates, which remained open until we came within a yard of them, when they were slammed in our faces."

'in the interests of one lady'. So Sophia came up with a plan: she placed notices in newspapers to recruit others, so that more than 'one lady' would apply along with her. Sophia and the six women she recruited were the first to enrol at any university in the UK. They became known as 'the Edinburgh Seven'. Sophia wrote to a friend, "It is a grand thing to enter the very first British university ever opened to women, isn't it?"

> **"It is a grand thing to enter the very first British university ever opened to women, isn't it?"**

Although they were allowed to study medicine, Sophia and her friends had to pay higher fees, while male students who scored less than them in exams were awarded scholarships. They faced harassment from men angry that they were allowed to study: fireworks were attached to their doors, they were followed and shouted at in the street, and they were heckled when they walked into lessons. They even endured the Surgeons' Hall Riot. Despite the abuse, they carried on learning.

But Sophia was furious when Edinburgh University refused to award the Edinburgh Seven their degrees. She was granted her medical degree by the University of Berne, Switzerland, in 1877, so she could finally became the first practising female doctor in Scotland.

Thanks to the Edinburgh Seven, people in power were finally taking women's education seriously. A new law passed in 1877 ensured women could go to university in the UK and Ireland.

THE SURGEONS' HALL RIOT

The Surgeons' Hall Riot in 1870 was a pivotal moment for Sophia and the other members of the Edinburgh Seven. The women were trying to get into Surgeons' Hall to sit an anatomy exam when a 200-strong crowd blocked their path, pelting them with mud and rubbish. The gates were slammed in their faces. Sympathetic students and janitors finally reopened the gates so they could sit their exam. This shocking incident led to a surge in public support for the Edinburgh Seven.

Sophia went on to found both the Edinburgh Hospital and Dispensary for Women and Children, and the Edinburgh School of Medicine, where she taught women like Elsie Inglis studying to become doctors (read about Elsie on p. 74). And finally, as a result of Sophia's campaigning, in 1894 the University of Edinburgh began allowing women to graduate with degrees in medicine. Sophia strongly believed in empowering women, and her determination dramatically improved women's healthcare in Scotland.

THE EDINBURGH SEVEN

The Edinburgh Seven – Sophia Jex-Blake, Mary Anderson, Emily Bovell, Matilda Chaplin, Helen Evans, Edith Pechey and Isabel Thorne – were awarded their medical degrees from the University of Edinburgh in 2019, 149 years after the Surgeons' Hall Riot.

EMELI SANDÉ
Musician and Singer-songwriter
Born Sunderland, England, 1987

Emeli grew up in Alford, Aberdeenshire, with her sister, white English mum and Zambian dad. She enjoyed family trips to the river and exploring the countryside, but most of all she had a passion for music. The family listened to traditional Scottish music at ceilidhs, and her father introduced her to a range of musicians, including soul singer Nina Simone and Zambian artists.

At primary school, Emeli learned several instruments, including recorder, clarinet and piano, and sang in the school choir. She wrote her first song aged 11 for a school talent show. Throughout her teens, she entered nationwide competitions for undiscovered talent and made an impression: at 16, she was offered a record contract in London.

MAKING A NAME FOR HERSELF

Emeli's real first name is Adele, but she started using her middle name because when she was at university, the English singer Adele broke on to the music scene. Emeli thought two singers called Adele would be confusing!

But education was important to Emeli and her family, and she had worked hard to be accepted to study medicine at the University of Glasgow. She chose to go to university and music took a back seat. Yet while doing her course, she still wrote and performed music in her

spare time. After three years – during which she gained a degree in neuroscience, the study of how the brain works – she realised she really wanted to be a musician after all. She let go of medicine, moved to London and started building her music career.

"Leaving university was hard," Emeli remembers. "I was taking a risk. But my passion for music was so strong that I knew I was following my heart."

The risk was worth it: Emeli's style of R&B, pop and soul was a massive success. In 2012, Emeli's first album *Our Version of Events* spent ten weeks at No. 1 and was the best-selling album of the year. Later, it became the eighth best-selling album of the decade. She says, "That makes me very proud. It's probably my biggest achievement." Emeli has also had 15 UK Top 40 singles, including two No. 1s, and three more albums called *Long Live the Angels*, *Real Life* and *Let's Say for Instance*.

OLYMPIC TRIBUTE

For Emeli, the highlight of her musical breakthrough in 2012 was singing at the opening ceremony of the Olympic Games in London. Her performance was a tribute to people who had died in a terrorist attack in the city five years earlier. Alone on stage, knowing that 900 million people were watching on TV, she took a deep breath and sang the hymn 'Abide With Me' as dancers below her performed a stunning routine.

"I was very nervous," Emeli recalls. "It was a quiet moment in the show and so important to so many people. I'm just thankful that it went well."

EMELI THE SONGWRITER

Emeli has written songs for other artists too, including Alicia Keys, Katy Perry and Rihanna.

Emeli has faced challenges too. She explains, "Sadly sexism and racism have been big barriers for me. It's important to read about both, because often you don't realise that something is racism. The more I learn, the better I am able to deal with it."

Emeli has never regretted choosing to do what she loves. There is no guarantee of success with a performing career but, as Emeli says, "That's what's so exciting about music!"

"My passion for music was so strong that I knew I was following my heart."

BIG BRIT WINNER

Emeli has won four Brit awards. In 2012, she won the Critics' Choice, and in 2013, she won British Female Solo Artist, and British Album of the Year. In 2017, she was again named British Female Solo Artist.

KAREN GILLAN
Actor
Born Inverness, 1987

Karen always wanted to be an actor and film-maker. When she was little, she remembers, "I had a lot of alone time, with no brothers or sisters running around. I would just sit and imagine things, all the time." She would use her mum's video camera to shoot pretend movies. She liked horror films and her poor dad would end up covered in tomato-sauce fake blood!

Karen lived in Inverness, a long way from the UK's movie hub, London, but she was very determined. Aged 15, she wrote to every agent in Scotland asking for help to develop her career. She moved to Edinburgh to study an HNC in Acting and Performance at Telford College, then to London to the Italia Conti Academy of Theatre Arts.

Karen picked up small parts in television shows, then at the age of 21 she landed her breakthrough role: Amy Pond, the main companion to Matt Smith's Time Lord in the hugely popular TV series *Doctor Who*. Soon Karen was being recognised in the street and asked for selfies by fans. She played Amy for three years. She says, "*Doctor Who* was the result of years of work and I felt ready for everything that came with it."

After *Doctor Who*, Karen moved to Los Angeles. She starred in horror movie *Oculus*,

DOCTOR TWO

Karen appeared as a soothsayer in an episode of *Doctor Who* two years before she played Amy Pond.

"Acting is all about finding the truth within whatever world you're in."

Aged 15, she wrote to every agent in Scotland asking for help to develop her career.

and then achieved global fame playing Nebula in Marvel superhero film *Guardians of the Galaxy*. To accomplish Nebula's many combat scenes, Karen began strength training and weight-lifting. She spent time with the stunt crew learning martial arts choreography so she could do as many of her own stunts as possible. One fight scene could sometimes take four days to film! Karen also shaved her head and spent five gruelling hours each day having prosthetic make-up applied and large contact lenses fitted to achieve Nebula's distinctive cyborg look. Karen is also famous for another hit series, the *Jumanji* movies, where she puts her fighting skills to good use playing the character Ruby Roundhouse.

MARVELLOUS KAREN

Karen is a vital part of one of cinema's biggest franchises, the Marvel Cinematic Universe. In the Marvel movies, Karen has worked with some of Hollywood's biggest stars, including Scarlett Johansson, Brie Larson, Zoe Saldana and Gwyneth Paltrow. So far she has played Nebula in six films: *Guardians of the Galaxy Volumes 1, 2* and *3, Thor: Love and Thunder, Avengers: Infinity War* and *Avengers: Endgame*, which from 2019 to 2021 was the highest-grossing film of all time.

Karen never forgot her desire to make films as well as star in them. She directed two short films, *Coward* and *Confidence*, to gain experience before tackling a full-length film, saying, "Directing is a completely different job from acting. It was really, really informative and helpful to just practise. Like anything, you get better at it, and you start to learn more about your individuality and style as a film-maker." And in 2017 she returned home to Inverness to write, direct and act in an independent film called *The Party's Just Beginning*. It was nominated as Best Feature Film at the Scottish Bafta awards.

There are relatively few women directors in the film and TV industry, and Karen, reflecting on her film-making experience, says, "I do hope it will inspire more young film-makers, particularly female ones. That they'll think about it as a potential career. It's possible!"

LAST CONTACT

Karen had to wear huge black contact lenses that covered her eyes to play Nebula. They were so uncomfortable that now she can't even wear normal-sized contact lenses any more.

HAIR, THERE AND EVERYWHERE

When Karen's long red hair was shaved for the role of Nebula, Marvel made it into a wig for her. She wore it on comedy series *Selfie* and in a *Doctor Who* Christmas special. Eventually she donated the wig to the make-up crew on *Star Wars: The Force Awakens*. Karen's hair has been all over the galaxy!

MARY SOMERVILLE

Mathematician, Astronomer, Scientist and Writer

Born Jedburgh, Scottish Borders, 1780

When Mary was young, she lived in Burntisland, Fife, where she would collect shells and fossils on the beach. She was fascinated by the movements of the stars and wanted to find out their secrets.

But in the eighteenth century, most people believed girls did not need an education. Mary was expected to help her mother look after the house and garden, and was only sent to school occasionally. She thought this was unfair, so decided to teach herself. Her father, a Navy captain, didn't earn a lot but he came from a well-off family and owned many books. Mary taught herself by eagerly reading books from the family library. An uncle helped her learn Latin, and later she devoured books on maths, algebra and astronomy, which is the science of planets and stars.

She grew up and got married, but her husband didn't

THE FIRST SCIENTIST

The word 'scientist' was invented to describe Mary by philosopher William Whewell. Before that, people used to say 'man of science'.

"I thought it unjust that women should have been given a desire for knowledge if it were wrong to acquire it."

support her desire to learn. However, after he died, Mary married again, and this time her new husband, William Somerville, encouraged her to study physics, chemistry and geology. She balanced her work and family life, writing: "I rose early and made such arrangements with regard to my children and family affairs that I had time to write afterwards; not, however, without many interruptions. A man can always command his time under the plea of business, a woman is not allowed any such excuse."

Mary became one of the first women elected as an Honorary Member of the Royal Astronomical Society.

MARY THE CAMPAIGNER

Throughout her whole life, Mary stood against many kinds of injustice. As a child, she refused sugar in her tea because it was grown using slave labour. Even when Mary became famous and respected, she never forgot how unjust it felt not to be allowed to go to school regularly simply because she was a girl, and she became a powerful voice for women's rights. When John Stuart Mill, a well-known philosopher and economist, organised a petition calling on Parliament to allow women to vote, Mary was the first person to sign.

During decades of research, Mary contributed to scientific debates and gradually became well known in Scotland and England, earning the respect of the scientific community. At 51, Mary published her first book, *Mechanism of the Heavens*, which explained astronomy to ordinary readers.

MARY + ADA = FRIENDS

Mary tutored – and became good friends with – Ada Lovelace, who was a skilled mathematician and helped invent the world's first computer.

Mary became one of the first women elected as an Honorary Member of the Royal Astronomical Society. With careful scientific observation, she spotted something strange in the movement of the planet Uranus and suggested the cause was interference from another, unknown planet. Thanks to her pioneering work, Neptune was discovered in 1848.

Time and again, Mary proved that science was not just for men. Nine years after her death, Somerville Hall – established for women studying at the University of Oxford – was named after her. Mary was a trailblazer for women and girls in the sciences.

CELEBRATING SOMERVILLE

Mary's work and achievements are widely recognised today. She is the face of the Royal Bank of Scotland's £10 note and even has a crater named after her on the moon.

LORRAINE KELLY

Journalist and Broadcaster

Born the Gorbals, Glasgow, 1959

When Lorraine was growing up in the Gorbals area of Glasgow, she loved listening to other people's stories, especially those told by her mum and gran. "Some people would say the women in my family are nosey, but I like to say we're inquisitive," she explains. "Stories have always been a big part of my life."

Lorraine was a keen learner, and her parents taught her to read and write before she went to school. Although her family was working class, Lorraine says, "I was bullied slightly because, unbelievably, the other kids said I was posh. It was because my mum had me turned out like a princess! But I enjoyed school and worked hard."

When Lorraine was 17 she spotted an advert for a junior reporter job at her local newspaper, *East Kilbride News*. She says, "It was like a lightbulb going off in my mind – I just knew that was what I wanted to do."

RUSSIAN AROUND

Lorraine turned down a place at university to study English and Russian so she could begin her first reporter job, but she went on to learn Russian anyway.

Lorraine

"My job is never about me, it's about who I'm talking to and what they are telling me."

"Sometimes life takes you in a different direction than you'd planned, and that's alright!"

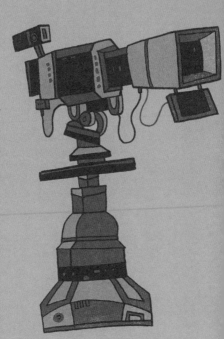

Lorraine got the job, and later moved to the BBC as a researcher. After being told that she needed to change her accent to be a successful broadcaster, she moved to rival ITV's popular morning show *TV-am* to be their Scottish correspondent. She says, "The day after I'd been told I needed elocution lessons, I applied for the *TV-am* job. It gave me the kick to do it. Sometimes life takes you in a different direction than you'd planned, and that's alright!"

TELLING SCOTLAND'S STORIES

As a journalist, Lorraine has covered some of the UK's most important stories. She reported on the Lockerbie bombing in 1989, when a plane exploded above the Dumfriesshire town, and also on the Dunblane massacre: a primary school shooting in Dunblane, near Stirling, in 1996. "There are some stories that never leave you," she says. "I covered Lockerbie when I was young and I was still learning. I did get involved emotionally with Dunblane, but it was a huge honour and privilege that people trusted me to tell their stories."

ACTING UP

Lorraine has made cameo acting appearances in TV programmes like *River City* and *Still Game*.

Lorraine uses her platform to fundraise for as many good causes as she can, like breast cancer charities and Help for Heroes, which supports injured military veterans. In 2011, she also took part in the Red Nose Desert Trek across the Kaisut Desert for Comic Relief. She and other celebrities trekked 100km, raising £1.3 million. She says, "I'm so happy to help. If I can make a difference, then that's wonderful."

For 35 years, millions of viewers have watched Lorraine on breakfast telly. Her warm, chatty manner puts guests at ease and has made her one of Britain's best-loved presenters. And she still loves listening to other people's stories.

BREAKFAST DOMINATION

Lorraine's breakfast TV shows have included *GMTV*, *Daybreak* and *Lorraine*, and she has a special award from Bafta Scotland to recognise 30 years in television.

JEANNIE ROBERTSON

Traditional Folk Singer

Born Aberdeen, 1908

Jeannie was the youngest of five children, and her family were part of the Traveller community in north-east Scotland. Her dad died when she was a baby and her mother remarried. Music and poetry was a big part of the family's life.

They spent cold winters living in a house in Aberdeen, but when the first glimmers of spring were felt in the air, the family went from place to place in their caravan. Jeannie spent her summers fruit-picking in Blairgowrie, Perthshire. She loved the freedom of being on the road and the sense of community with other Traveller families. At night, they would gather round the campfire and sing traditional songs. Jeannie and her sisters listened closely as their mother taught them the stories behind the songs.

Aged 20, Jeannie married Donald Higgins, a talented piper. They carried on the Traveller tradition of staying in Aberdeen in winter, in a tenement in Causeway End (or 'Cassieend'), where they often hosted ceilidhs. Jeannie's incredible voice was becoming famous in the north-east, and she made up her own songs as she did her housework.

Jeannie kept heritage alive that may otherwise have been completely lost.

"Ma mither an' her brother used to sing the songs thigether ... The auld songs went frae mooth tae mooth in these days."

MUSICAL FAMILY

Jeannie had many musical relatives. Her aunt was also a singer, her nephew was a storyteller, singer and piper, and her daughter released an album too.

Around the same time, Jeannie heard Scottish poet Hamish Henderson talking to American folklorist Alan Lomax on the radio about folk songs. She said, "If those men only kent to come to Cassieend, I cud give them a few auld sangs."

Soon, Hamish *did* knock on her door. He had come searching for songs in Aberdeen and been told of Jeannie. Once she sang, he realised her talent and discovered she knew hundreds of traditional songs. Hamish began to record and promote her work, and attended her home ceilidhs, where he collected numerous songs and stories. Jeannie appeared on BBC radio, was interviewed by newspapers, and began performing to a younger, UK-wide audience.

CHALLENGING STEREOTYPES

Jeannie and fellow members of the Traveller community faced a lot of prejudice. Many people believed in offensive stereotypes about Travellers, and still do today. But Jeannie was very proud of her heritage, and her songs helped people to understand the Traveller way of life.

JEANNIE ROBERTSON

In 1968, Jeannie was awarded an MBE for services to folksong, making history as both the first Traveller and the first folk singer to be honoured. But she always felt her greatest achievement was sharing her songs with the world as a tradition-bearer. By passing them to not only her own children and nephew but also recording them for future generations worldwide, she kept heritage alive that may otherwise have been completely lost. The Scottish Traditional Music Hall of Fame calls her 'a monumental figure in Scottish traditional song whose influence and importance as a preserver of folklore will sustain for as long as traditional songs are sung'.

FAMOUS SONGS

Jeannie's most celebrated songs are 'I'm A Man Youse Don't Meet Every Day' (which was covered by the band The Pogues) and 'Son David'.

JEANNIE'S WORDS

Auld = old

Kent = knew or known

Mither = mother

Cud = could

Mooth = mouth

Thigither = together

LIZ McCOLGAN

Athlete

Born Dundee, 1964

Liz grew up in Whitfield, Dundee, an area where many people lived in poverty. She loved sport, but her family could not afford to pay for classes. Instead she went to as many free after-school clubs as she could, including gymnastics, hockey, netball and volleyball. When she went to high school, her PE teacher was a marathon runner and would make his classes run cross-country during winter. He recognised Liz had a talent for running and persuaded her to join Dundee Hawkhill Harriers athletic club when she was 13.

"To know you are the best at any one point in time is pretty special."

"I went three times a week and it became my life," Liz says. "I loved it because running gave me something to focus on other than the problems we faced because of where we lived. I wasn't dreaming of becoming a champion."

Yet by the time Liz left school, her athletics coach, Harry Bennett, was convinced she had champion potential. Liz explains, "I was working in a jute mill from 7 a.m. until 5 p.m., so I'd get up early and go for a run, or we'd train at lunchtime. It was very difficult, but Harry encouraged me."

When Liz was offered a scholarship to train at an American university, she finally started believing in herself: "I knew then I could be the best." Yet her family could not afford the plane ticket. Harry paid for her to go.

After four years winning track titles in the USA, Liz ran the 10,000m in the 1986 Commonwealth Games in Edinburgh – and won gold. She remembers, "As the laps went by, the crowd knew something was going to happen. The atmosphere was building and the last two laps were manic. I won that medal in front of my home crowd, in front of my family. It was the most emotional win of my life."

GOING FOR GOLD

Liz ran longer distances too, winning marathons in New York in 1991, Tokyo in 1992 and London in 1996. She says, "It's hard to say which was the best, but winning in front of a home crowd in London was a big dream of mine."

Next Liz turned her attention towards the Olympic Games, and in 1988 won a silver medal in the 10,000m in Seoul. She successfully defended her Commonwealth title in New Zealand in 1990.

But Liz faced huge challenges before her next championship. Her sponsor, Nike, cancelled her contract after she told them she was pregnant. This meant Liz was no longer being paid, and it led to huge financial worry for her. Liz remembers, "Nike thought I wouldn't come back and be successful, and that was the way they dealt with it at the time." With only three days to go before her World Championship race in Tokyo, Asics stepped in to sponsor her.

And on a hot, humid night in Japan at the 1991 World Championships, Liz became the best in the world, winning the 10,000m just nine months after having a baby. She says, "That race was probably one of the toughest that's ever been run in a championship. The conditions were hard, the competition was very high, and the way that I ran it was bold, because I ran from the front. To know you are the best at any one point in time is pretty special. I felt amazing."

Liz's World Championship gold proved sportswomen didn't need to end their careers to start a family. She reflects, "In my mind, I always knew I'd return. I was one of the first women to come back to their sport and be successful, and it led the way for a lot of other women."

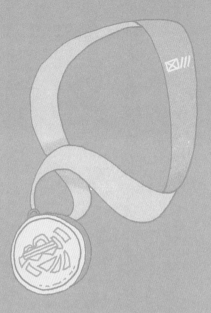

RUNS IN THE FAMILY

Liz coaches her daughter Eilish, who is also an exceptional athlete. Eilish smashed the British half-marathon record in 2022, and again in 2023 with a time of 1:05:43. That's even faster than her mum's half-marathon best of 1:07:11.

Eilish followed in her mum's footsteps when she won gold in a thrilling 10,000m race at the 2022 Commonwealth Games in Birmingham. And the following year she ran 10,000m in 30:00:86, beating her mum's Scottish record of 30:57:07!

JOAN EARDLEY

Artist

Born Warnham, England, 1921

Joan was brought up in a house full of women. She lived with her sister, mum, grandmother and aunt. Joan's aunt, a feminist who campaigned for peace and women's rights, was a big influence on her as a youngster.

At school in London, a teacher noted that Joan's drawings and paintings showed unusual promise, and her mum was supportive of her desire to become an artist. When Joan was 18, the family moved to Bearsden in Glasgow, and not long after that the Second World War broke out. In the early months of the war, Joan was accepted to study at the renowned Glasgow School of Art.

ART SCHOOL AND AIR RAIDS

Joan's start at Glasgow School of Art was delayed for several months because the Second World War had just begun and air-raid shelters were being built in the art school's basement.

After the war, she was awarded a scholarship to travel to Italy to paint. Joan was interested in everyday scenes. Instead of painting rich people, she portrayed fishermen by the sea and beggars in Venice, and used pastels to sketch animals.

Joan loved children, and when she returned home to Glasgow she spent hours sketching them playing in the city's streets. Children, especially those living in poverty, were not often

artists' subject matter. Many of the youngsters lived in slums, and Joan made sure she captured every aspect of their lives in her art, from their ragged clothes to their energetic games.

CAMOUFLAGE ARTIST

During the Second World War, Joan continued to study evening classes at the Glasgow School of Art. By day she worked for a firm that built boats, painting camouflage patterns on military vessels.

But painting children was not Joan's only strength. When she visited Catterline, a coastal fishing village on a grassy cliff in Aberdeenshire, the atmosphere and the unusual light intrigued her. She instantly wanted to paint the village. She gradually made Catterline her home.

Joan's work is some of Scotland's most admired and influential twentieth-century art.

Joan would transport her materials to the beach on her scooter and use rocks to secure her canvas. She would even paint the North Sea during storms, as it was whipped up by the wind. Sometimes sand would stick to the paint and she would work it into the picture. She also used grass, petals and seeds, just as she glued collages of objects like sweet

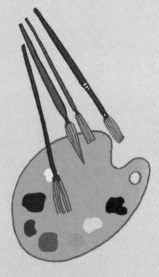

wrappers into her pictures of children. She once said, "I don't know what I'm painting... I'm just trying to paint."

JOAN IN CATTERLINE

Children used to watch Joan painting on the beach in Catterline, intrigued by her. Although she portrayed children in Glasgow, she didn't paint them in Catterline, concentrating instead on capturing the landscape. She was very tolerant of the onlooking children and would hand them sweets before politely telling them she had work to do.

Joan's cottage in Catterline had no heating or running water. Locals there grew to love and respect her, and were proud to call her one of their own. When she became too unwell to paint outside, her friends brought wildflowers to her cottage and she created still-life portraits of the blooms to feel connected to nature.

Sadly, Joan died of breast cancer aged 42, but her work is some of Scotland's most admired and influential twentieth-century art. A large exhibition marking 100 years since her birth toured in 2021, and Joan's paintings are regularly on display in all the nation's major galleries, inspiring new generations of artists.

ROZA SALIH

Human Rights Activist and Councillor

Born Sulaymaniyah, Iraq, 1989

When Roza was 12 she arrived in her new home, a tower-block flat in Glasgow, and she couldn't believe the constant rain. The weather was grey, but she and her Kurdish family were finally safe.

They had come to Glasgow from Iraq. It was 2001 and they had left their home to seek asylum because they had opposed brutal Iraqi ruler Saddam Hussein. His regime had executed her grandfather and two uncles, and Roza's dad feared he could be next.

"I like being able to give people a voice."

The Salih family were placed in a flat in Glasgow's Knightswood area. Roza felt they stood out from everyone else, remembering, "I didn't speak a word of English and we were discriminated against. We had vouchers to use in the supermarket; we couldn't use cash. It was very stigmatising." This made Roza feel unequal and ashamed.

Roza was a pupil at Drumchapel High School. One day in 2005, her friend Agnesa wasn't in class. Roza says, "Me and Ewelina, another friend, knew something was wrong. We found out Agnesa had been taken to Yarl's Wood, a detention centre in England for asylum seekers. They wanted to deport her to Kosovo."

Roza and her friends felt the UK government had made the wrong decision and treated their friend terribly, so they formed the Glasgow Girls.

Supported by their teacher Mr Girvan, and then the community around them, the Glasgow Girls wanted to highlight asylum seekers' struggles and their treatment. They started with a petition in school, then raised public awareness. They spoke to journalists and politicians and took their fight to the Scottish Parliament.

WHAT IS AN ASYLUM SEEKER?

A person seeking asylum is someone who travels to another country looking for safety, for example, if they are likely to be harmed by their own government or army. The new country that asylum seekers travel to decides whether they need to stay.

At the time Roza was seeking asylum, UK immigration officers could take families seeking asylum by surprise, forcing their way into homes at night. This was known as a 'dawn raid'. Parents were handcuffed, and families – like Agnesa's – were taken to detention centres (like prisons), and then sent away from the UK.

The Glasgow Girls met the First Minister of Scotland at the time, Jack McConnell. Although the UK government was in charge of asylum-seekers, Mr McConnell promised that Scotland would try to treat them better. He assured the girls there would be no more dawn raids or detaining children. Agnesa's family were allowed to return to Scotland while their case was considered again, and in 2008 it was decided they could stay permanently. Roza says, "It didn't happen right away, but it did happen. Agnesa returned! We got her back."

When Roza left school, she studied law and politics at the University of Strathclyde, in Glasgow. In 2022 she made history by becoming the first refugee to be elected as a councillor in Scotland, for Glasgow City Council.

THE GLASGOW GIRLS

The seven Glasgow Girls were Roza, Amal Azzudin, Emma Clifford, Toni-Lee Henderson, Jennifer McCarron, Ewelina Siwak and Agnesa Murselaj herself. Their inspiring story was turned into a BBC Scotland musical television drama and a stage musical, both called *Glasgow Girls*.

Roza has also campaigned for workers' rights, Kurdish freedom and Scottish independence. She says, "The most important thing I've learned throughout my life is to always stick up for people. I like being able to give people a voice."

SCOTTISH SCHOLARSHIPS

Thanks to Roza's campaigning, Strathclyde became the first Scottish university to offer scholarships to people seeking asylum. Every other university in Scotland has since introduced a similar programme.

ELSIE INGLIS

Doctor and Suffragist

Born Nainital, India, 1864

Elsie was born in colonial India to a Scottish family and had a privileged upbringing with her siblings. Unusually for Victorian times, her parents believed that girls' education was just as important as boys', and they supported Elsie's ambition to be a doctor. She and her sister Eva would paint spots on dolls and treat them for pretend measles.

Elsie's parents returned to Edinburgh when she was 12, and she went on to study medicine there aged 23, in 1887. She qualified as a doctor at a time when this was very difficult for women. Shocked by poor standards of care for women and children, Elsie chose to work at hospitals in London and Dublin that focused on women's health. She had big plans, writing to her father: "I mean to have a hospital of my own in Edinburgh some day." And when she returned home, she did just that: she set up a maternity hospital for women in poverty.

When the First World War began, Elsie knew she had the skills to help injured soldiers. With financial support from the women's suffrage movement, she founded the Scottish Women's Hospitals for Foreign Service (SWH), a unit of nurses.

PASSING IT ON

Elsie began her medical studies at the Edinburgh School of Medicine for Women, set up by Sophia Jex-Blake, the first female practising doctor in Scotland. (Read more about Sophia on page 38.)

But when she offered their services to the government's War Office, she was told: "My good lady, go home and sit still."

Determined Elsie approached other Allied forces, who were very grateful for her help. Eventually there were 1,500 SWH workers, all but 20 of them women, serving as doctors, surgeons, nurses, ambulance drivers, orderlies and cooks. They set up 17 units and provided medical support on battlefields across Europe, saving thousands of lives.

SUFFRAGIST SUPPORTER

Elsie was the secretary of the Edinburgh National Society for Women's Suffrage and later became honorary secretary for the Scottish Federation of Women's Suffrage Societies. 'Suffrage' means being able to vote in and stand as a candidate in political elections. These societies campaigned for women's right to vote.

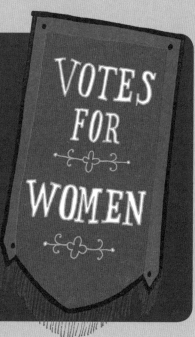

VOTES FOR WOMEN

"I mean to have a hospital of my own in Edinburgh some day."

Elsie spent most of the war as a doctor in Serbia. It was dangerous work, and she was even captured and became a prisoner of war for a time. The day after she arrived back in Britain, she died of cancer, with her family by her bedside.

Elsie's incredible legacy improved healthcare for women and showed the world that women were more than capable of doing professional work at a time when many people doubted this.

SAYING GOODBYE

Elsie's funeral was held at St Giles' Cathedral in Edinburgh. The streets were lined with mourners, mostly women. Her coffin was draped in the flags of the UK and Serbia, and was carried to her grave by Serbians.

ELSIE'S EDINBURGH LEGACY

The maternity hospital Elsie opened in Edinburgh was called The Hospice. Elsie often didn't charge the hospital's patients for treatment, because they were mainly poor women. At the time there was no NHS in Britain and medical treatment usually had to be paid for.

Elsie inspired others to give medical care to women and children too. In 1925, the Elsie Inglis Memorial Maternity Hospital in Edinburgh was named in her honour. Thousands of Edinburgh babies were born at "Elsie's" until it closed in 1988.

CATHERINE HEYMANS

Astrophysicist

Born Hitchin, England, 1978

"What's the hardest job in the world?" Catherine asked her nursery teacher, who replied, "Probably a brain surgeon or an astrophysicist." At that moment, Catherine knew she was either going to be a doctor or discover how the universe worked.

As she grew up in a quiet village just outside London, Catherine struggled to decide between physics and medicine, but a teacher helped make up her mind. "When I was 16 I had the most amazing, passionate physics teacher," she explains. Inspired, at 18 she started studying astrophysics at the University of Edinburgh.

Catherine says, "It's not like any other science where you can prod and poke; you can only see what the universe chooses to share with you. We can observe through our telescopes the hottest, densest regions of the universe, empty gigantic voids, cataclysmic events where black holes crash into each other, and we can explain them because of our understanding of physics."

SATURN ABOVE SCOTLAND

Catherine saw Saturn in the dark sky for the first time on a childhood trip to Scotland.

"In Scotland, we have a whole wilderness above us because we have pristine dark skies. Studying the sky above us is full of joy and surprises!"

During university she worked as a tour guide at the Royal Observatory, Edinburgh and at a bar, explaining physics during both jobs: "A lot of people are scared of science, but when I talked to them from behind the bar they realised how fascinating it is."

TALKING MATHS

Catherine's top tip to budding scientists is to work hard... at maths! She says, "It's really important to learn languages to communicate, and maths is the language of science."

After graduating with a first-class honours degree, Catherine became a lecturer and eventually a professor, specialising in the dark universe. In 2021, she became the first female Astronomer Royal for Scotland – based at the same observatory where she had once been a tour guide!

WANTED: FEMALE PHYSICISTS

Catherine was shocked when she went from her all girls' state school into astrophysics at university. "Out of sixty students, only six were female. I wasn't lectured by a single woman," she says. "Things are changing, but it's still too slow."

Catherine still believes in making science accessible, particularly to children, and campaigns for every outdoor activity centre in Scotland to have a telescope, so more people can watch the night sky. She believes, "If you make that connection, not on an iPad, not on telly, but with your own eyes looking through a telescope, then you'll take that home and push your parents into doing more cool science stuff."

She also wants to open up STEM careers. "We need people from as many different backgrounds as possible," she says. "When we make scientific breakthroughs, they typically come from someone who's looking at the big questions from another angle to everybody else."

"We need people from as many different backgrounds as possible."

A DIAMOND AS BIG AS THE MOON

One of Catherine's favourite fun facts about space is about our sun. She says: "Stars live and die like we do, and in billions of years, the sun will die and form a diamond about the size of the moon."

EXPLORING THE DARK UNIVERSE

Catherine is an expert on the dark universe, which is made up of dark matter and dark energy. Dark matter pulls the universe together, whereas dark energy forces the universe to expand. Catherine says: "Our theory is that surrounding each and every galaxy is a big clump of dark matter. You can't see it; it doesn't absorb or emit light; it's invisible stuff. But we think it has to be there, otherwise there's not enough gravity to keep the galaxies glued together. You need this extra stuff there. It's all a big mystery."

MARY BARBOUR

Social and Political Activist

Born Kilbarchan, Renfrewshire, 1875

Mary lived in a busy household with her parents and her six brothers and sisters. Kilbarchan was a weaving village, and when Mary grew up she trained in how to print designs onto carpets.

She married David Barbour when she was 21, and the couple moved to Govan, in Glasgow. There was not enough housing in the crowded city for everyone, and standards were terrible: people were crammed into dirty tenement flats in slums, and disease was rife.

After the First World War began in 1914, more workers piled into Glasgow to take jobs in factories. This made finding a place to live even harder, and the crisis worsened when landlords took advantage to increase rents by 25 per cent. With men away fighting on the frontline, landlords thought women wouldn't stand up to them.

But Mary hated injustice. She had campaigned against poverty and for women's voting rights before the war. She realised the power women could have when they stood together, and led the South Govan Women's Housing Association's struggle against greedy landlords. The women went on rent strike, plastering windows in posters that declared: "We are not paying increased rents." And when bailiffs turned up to force tenants out of their homes, 'Mrs Barbour's Army' was ready.

"Now that we have political power, we are determined to use it for the direction of securing healthy homes for ourselves and our children."

In the tenements, several flats shared a stairwell. One woman in a block would keep lookout so the other residents could get on with their daily lives. When the lookout saw the bailiffs approaching, she'd loudly ring a bell so the other women could barricade access to the close (the shared hallway) or pelt them with flour bombs and other missiles.

Mary and the other women pelted bailiffs with flour bombs.

RED CLYDESIDE

At the start of the twentieth century, Glasgow was a global centre of ship-building, engineering and other heavy industries. Lots of people in the city worked in these industries, which were often based on the banks of the River Clyde. But in 1915, a series of disputes started between workers in factories and the government. These disputes became known as Red Clydeside.

Mary's rent strikes were an early and important part of Red Clydeside. Her campaign's success encouraged workers in factories to strike when the government tried to bring unskilled workers into the skilled workforce, threatening their jobs.

Red Clydeside and its protests radicalised lots of people in Glasgow. That means they came together to take direct action to change their working and living conditions for the better. Mary inspired many people to challenge the authorities in order to improve their lives.

By October 1915, 20,000 households in Glasgow were refusing to pay high rents and the unrest was spreading to other cities. The government was forced to pass a law that put rents back to pre-war levels. Mrs Barbour's Army had beaten the landlords!

Mary went on to join the Women's International League and, in 1916, co-founded the Women's Peace Crusade to campaign against the First World War. After the war ended in 1918, Mary's activism made her a natural political candidate. In 1920, she and four others – Eleanor Stewart, Jessica Baird-Smith, Mary Anderson Snodgrass and Mary Bell – became the first women to be elected to Glasgow's council.

As a councillor, Mary fought for changes that would improve the lives of women and children. She opened Scotland's first family-planning clinic and provided free milk for school children. She also campaigned against slum housing.

In 1924, Mary became Glasgow council's first woman Baillie (an important town officer) and was one of the first women magistrates (a kind of judge) in the city. Mary's pioneering work made a huge difference to many Glaswegians' lives and inspired other women to get involved in politics.

HONOURING MARY

After a long campaign to recognise Mary's achievements, a statue of her was unveiled in Govan in 2018. Her image is also on a mural near Glasgow city centre.

ANNE LORNE GILLIES

Gaelic Activist, Singer and Teacher

Born Stirlingshire, 1944

When Anne was five, her family moved to a croft in Oban, Argyll. She looked after cows, hens and geese, made hay, thinned turnips and pulled up potatoes. There was no electricity or running water, and they had to use an outside toilet, but Anne loved the freedom.

> "I began singing on telly... though we still didn't have electricity at home and I had never seen a television!"

Preserving traditional Highland language and culture was important to Anne's parents and they were delighted when a woman called Mrs Lawrie offered to help on the croft. "She spoke very little English," Anne explains, "but my mother wanted her to speak Gaelic to us, and she sang Gaelic songs."

Oban High School was a vibrant hub of Gaelic culture. The Hebridean islanders who studied there had grown up speaking Gaelic as a first language. Gaelic poet Iain Crichton Smith taught English at the school, and the head teacher was John Maclean, brother of the renowned Gaelic poet Sorley Maclean. While Anne studied there, she became fluent in Gaelic.

Anne also played piano and sang, and at 17 she won the Women's Gold Medal at the Mòd, an annual event that celebrates Gaelic culture. "I began singing on telly and radio," she says, "though we still didn't have electricity at home and I had hardly seen a television!"

SATURDAY-NIGHT STAR

Anne was a television star and appeared on popular Saturday-night show *Mainly Magnus* as the resident singer from 1971 to 1972. She was given her own one-off fifty-minute show, and it was so popular that a further six episodes were made.

She combined studying music and teacher training at university with her singing career – and always performed at least one Gaelic song. Anne captivated audiences in folk clubs, theatres, concerts and on radio. She became a big television star too.

Anne's appearances on TV brought Gaelic to a wider audience, but she knew that the importance of the language both in Scotland and around the world needed more official recognition. She became an important part of a campaign to protect and develop Gaelic.

PLAY BUS

Anne raised funds to buy a bus, painted it brightly and made it into a mobile Gaelic playgroup called Pàdraig am Bus Trang (Peter the Busy Bus).

Anne started to focus on education as patron of Comhairle nan Sgoiltean Àraich (the Gaelic Playgroup Association), and translated 50 songs and nursery rhymes for them. In the 1980s, Anne became a primary teacher and helped set up Glasgow's first classes in which children were taught in Gaelic. Gaelic-medium education is now an established and thriving part of the Scottish schooling system, with over 4,000 pupils. Anne also trained other teachers, and published Gaelic children's books and educational resources.

For her wide-ranging career encompassing singing, campaigning and teaching, the Scottish Traditional Music Hall of Fame has hailed Anne as 'one of the greatest champions of Gaelic culture'.

GAELIC IN SCOTLAND

Gaelic has been spoken in Scotland for 1,500 years. Yet since the eighteenth century there have been fewer and fewer Gaelic speakers. The Highland Clearances drove many Gaelic speakers to other countries. The British government tried to discourage Gaelic and make people use English instead. In 1872 speaking Gaelic in schools was banned.

Then in the late twentieth century, a big effort began to save the language from disappearing. The Gaelic Language (Scotland) Act was passed by the Scottish Parliament in 2005, to protect and promote the language and culture. Around 60 schools in Scotland now offer Gaelic-medium education.

The Gaelic words on p. 87 are lyrics from 'O Mo Dhùthaich (Oh My Country)', a traditional song performed by Anne Lorne Gillies. They mean: 'Oh my country, you are on my mind.'

FLORA MACDONALD

Jacobite Hero

Born Milton, South Uist, 1722

Flora, a member of Clan MacDonald of Sleat, grew up on the Hebridean Islands in the 1700s. Life on the islands was quiet, but the situation in mainland Scotland was very different.

Rival sides were fighting about who should be king. One side, the Jacobites, passionately believed Charles Edward Stuart – known as Bonnie Prince Charlie – should replace King George II, because they thought the prince had a stronger claim to the throne. But the Jacobite army was heavily defeated by the king's forces at the Battle of Culloden.

Flora, the prince and six others made the dangerous voyage to the Isle of Skye.

Bonnie Prince Charlie survived, and went on the run. Many Highlanders and Islanders hid him. Despite a £30,000 reward for his capture, an enormous amount of money at the time, no one gave him away. The prince was chased to Benbecula, where 24-year-old Flora was living. A Jacobite captain who was a distant relative of Flora's asked if she would help Bonnie Prince Charlie escape the island even though Flora was not a supporter of the Jacobites. At first she refused, fearing that her family could be punished. But when the prince himself asked, she took pity on him and agreed.

"I would have helped anyone who needed help."

Speed Bonnie Boat,
like a bird on the wing,
Over the sea to Skye.

They came up with a daring plan. Flora would travel alongside the prince, who would disguise himself as Betty Burke, her maid. Flora and a friend sewed the prince's costume. The authorities were so desperate to find him that people needed permission to leave the islands. Flora took a risk and asked her stepfather, a government official, to arrange the permits. So Flora, the prince and six others made the dangerous voyage to the Isle of Skye.

Bonnie Prince Charlie travelled onwards and eventually escaped to France. But Flora was arrested, sent to the Tower of London, and jailed for a year.

SING ME A SONG

Flora and Bonnie Prince Charlie never met again after saying goodbye in Skye. Their daring escape is remembered in the lyrics of 'The Skye Boat Song'. The song's chorus goes:

Speed, bonnie boat, like a bird on the wing,
Onward, the sailors cry,
Carry the lad who's born to be king,
Over the sea to Skye.

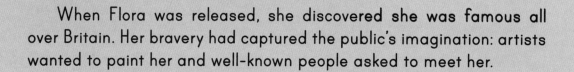

When Flora was released, she discovered she was famous all over Britain. Her bravery had captured the public's imagination: artists wanted to paint her and well-known people asked to meet her.

Flora's adventures weren't over. She got married and, later, in 1774, emigrated with her family to North Carolina. They were caught up in the American War of Independence and her husband was captured during battle. Flora eventually returned to her beloved Hebrides and spent the rest of her life there.

THE PRINCE'S GIFT

Bonnie Prince Charlie gave Flora a snuffbox (a small container to hold tobacco), inscribed with the words, 'A gift from Prince Charles Stewart to Miss Flora Macdonald 1746'. It is now in the National Museum of Scotland, donated by Flora's clan descendants.

GRAVE INSCRIPTION

The inscription on Flora's gravestone in Kilmuir, Skye, says, 'Her name will be mentioned in history, and if courage and fidelity be virtues, mentioned with honour.'

ALI SMITH
Author and Playwright
Born Inverness, 1962

Ali was the youngest of five children in a working-class family and grew up in a council house in Inverness. She loved nature and helped look after ponies at local stables, but reading and writing were her favourite things to do. There were always plenty of books to read at home. She remembers reading "everything in the house, including what my older siblings had in their school-book cupboard". She could never have imagined that one day she would be celebrated as one of the country's most important writers and her own books would be read all over the world.

Ali's love of books led to a first-class degree in English language and literature from the University of Aberdeen. She began a PhD at the University of Cambridge but decided not to continue, so she could focus on her writing. She had won a poetry prize in Aberdeen, and her first play, *Stalemate*, was staged at the Edinburgh Fringe Festival when she was just 24.

After being diagnosed with chronic fatigue syndrome, Ali gave up a lecturing job at the University of Strathclyde. She moved back to Cambridge with her partner,

AUTHOR OR SCAFFIE?

When Ali was little, she thought being a refuse collector – or a 'scaffie', as she called it – would be a fun job, as she would be able to reuse the things other people threw away.

"You never know what you're going to end up with when you sit down to write something."

Ali Smith Spring
Ali Smith Summer
Ali Smith Autumn
Ali Smith Winter

TURNING READING UPSIDE-DOWN

Ali's novel *How to Be Both* is unusual because it contains two halves printed in random order. So one reader will read the character George's story first and another will read Francesco's first, depending which copy of the book they pick up.

film-maker Sarah Wood, and gave the energy she had to writing. Her first short story collection, *Free Love and Other Stories*, was published when she was 28 and was an immediate success, winning the Saltire First Book of the Year and the Scottish Arts Council Book Award. Two years later, she released her debut novel, *Like*.

"Tell the right stories and we live better lives."

Ali has published many plays and short story collections, and more than ten novels. Relationships, art and the passing of time are recurring themes in Ali's work, and she often writes about love, sexuality and gender. Ali's work is regarded as some of the most important fiction written in twenty-first-century Britain. She is also popular – her recent novels have all been bestsellers.

Literary scholars find Ali's work interesting because she experiments with the way novels are written. Her books are regularly shortlisted for major literary prizes in English: *How to Be Both* won the Baileys Women's Prize for Fiction, the Folio Prize, the Goldsmiths Prize and the Costa Book Award for Novels, and was shortlisted for the Man Booker Prize. Ali has also won the Whitbread Novel of the Year and the Orwell Prize for Political Fiction.

The girl from Inverness who read as much as she could became a woman who pushed the boundaries of literature. "Tell the right stories," Ali says, "and we live better lives."

THE SEASONAL QUARTET

In 2016, Ali published *Autumn*, the first in her quartet of books named after the seasons. *Winter* followed in 2017, *Spring* in 2019 and finally *Summer* in 2020. Unusually for novels, these books were published very quickly after they had been written and reflected current events, like Donald Trump's presidency in the United States, Brexit and the COVID-19 pandemic.

SUPPORTING YOUNG PEOPLE

Ali is deeply concerned about the climate crisis, and writes about it in the Seasonal Quartet. She admires the way young people have taken the lead in highlighting the dangers of climate change and is a big fan of Swedish activist Greta Thunberg. "This young generation is amazing," Ali says. "They're showing us we need to change and we can change."

EUNICE OLUMIDE

Supermodel and Activist

Born Edinburgh, 1987

Eunice grew up with her Nigerian mum on a council estate in Wester Hailes, Edinburgh. When Eunice wasn't working hard at school, she hung out with friends and took long walks along the Union Canal. However, some people made racist comments, which badly affected her sense of self-worth. "Where I grew up, there wasn't anybody who looked like me," Eunice reflects. "I was probably the first black person a lot of people had met."

FRUITY FLAVOURS

When she was a child, Eunice's favourite sweets were Starbursts. She refused to eat fruit until her mum told her Nigeria's equivalent of Starbursts were mangoes!

When Eunice was asked to model as a teenager, she wasn't sure. She found it hard to believe it could be a real job for her, because she'd never seen models in magazines who looked like she did. "I was scouted five times before I gave it a go," she says, "but then it helped me to feel confident about my appearance, as I had very low self-esteem growing up."

Once she started, Eunice quickly became successful. She travelled all over the world for photoshoots,

Eunice has campaigned for Afro-Scottish history to be taught in schools.

working with top British fashion labels like Vivienne Westwood and Mulberry, and featuring in fashion magazines including *Harper's Bazaar* and *Tatler*. Modelling was fun, but Eunice had other ambitions too. Alongside her career in the fashion industry, she studied communications and media at Glasgow Caledonian University.

As she grew older, Eunice felt driven to use her fame to campaign against racism and change racist attitudes. She says, "Activism wasn't something I chose; it was more something I noticed needed to be done." Eunice has campaigned for Afro-Scottish history to be taught in schools to help Scotland understand its past, explaining, "Through education, people can understand why people of colour are present in their communities and what their huge contribution to society has been."

INVITING DISCUSSION

In 2017, Eunice was given an award called an MBE (Member of the Order of the British Empire) for services to art, broadcasting and charity work. She was unsure whether to accept because of the award's association with the British Empire and its connections to the slave trade. But she said yes after deciding to donate the MBE to the National Museum of Scotland to inspire discussion.

Eunice also supports charities that work against racism. In 2020, she set up the African Diaspora Business Support Fund to help entrepreneurs and businesses from black and minority ethnic backgrounds, saying, "It is so important to me to give back to my community, as I know what it's like to have nothing." Eunice says she wants to help make the world a better place: "I've always wanted to use my platform to empower others. My priority has always been to help people."

ROLE MODEL

Eunice mentors young people, and wrote a book called *How to Get into Fashion* for aspiring models, to guide them through their careers.

EUNICE OF ALL TRADES

Eunice has combined her very successful modelling career with many other kinds of work. As an actor, she appeared in *Star Wars: The Last Jedi* and *Rogue One: A Star Wars Story*, as well as the BBC adaptation of Malorie Blackman's classic novel *Noughts and Crosses*. She is a television presenter and broadcaster, has DJ'd all over the globe, and helped found the O Gallery in London, becoming one of few women of colour to have a leading role in the fine art industry.

JENNIE LEE

Politician

Born Lochgelly, Fife, 1904

Jennie's father, James, was a miner, and her mum, Euphemia, ran a hotel. As a child she was surrounded by her father's socialist friends, who wanted a fairer society, and her mum's friends, who worked in the theatre. Jennie grew up with a love of performance and art and a strong desire to help the working classes.

Jennie's parents expected her to leave school at 14 and start working, but she convinced them to let her stay. She became the dux (top of her year) and was the first in her family to go to university. In the 1920s hardly any women went on to higher education, but Jennie gained a law degree, a Master of Arts and a teaching diploma.

She became a teacher but later decided the best way she could help people in poverty was by getting elected to Parliament and making laws that would improve their lives. In 1929, age 25, she was elected as a Labour MP for North Lanarkshire – despite being too young to vote herself! Women had only been allowed to vote since 1918 and they had to be over 30.

> Jennie believed in the power of education to lift people out of poverty and transform lives.

The House of Commons could be intimidating and boisterous, but Jennie was never daunted. As an MP, she voted against her own political party when

ARTS FOR ALL

LEARN
AND
LIVE

THE PEOPLE'S CHAMPION

"There it is – a great, independent university which does not insult any man or woman, whatever their background, by offering them the second best. Nothing but the best is good enough."

Labour introduced dental and prescription charges in the 1950s. She felt charging people for medical treatment went against everything the National Health Service stood for. She also rebelled when, later in life, she became Baroness Lee of Asheridge in the House of Lords – and voted to abolish the House of Lords!

WINNING AND LOSING

The life of an MP can be unpredictable. Jennie lost her seat in North Lanarkshire in 1931. She was later re-elected in 1945 as MP for Cannock and remained its MP until 1970, when she entered the House of Lords.

Jennie believed in the power of education to lift people out of poverty and transform lives. When she became Minister for the Arts in 1964, she helped create the Open University, which taught adults of all ages in many different situations, rather than just school-leavers. She faced a lot of opposition, even within her own

SUPPORTING THE ARTS

As Minister for the Arts, Jennie trebled the Arts Council's budget in six years. She made sure opera, ballet, theatre and museum projects were supported all over the UK, not just in London, saying, "I deeply resented any idea that there was a certain level of perfection for a few well-heeled people and that anything was good enough for the rest."

party, but she was determined to make higher education accessible. Prime Minister Harold Wilson backed her plan.

The Open University was founded in 1969, and by 2019 it had educated two million people, including 200,000 Scots. The institution honoured Jennie by naming buildings after her at its Milton Keynes campus and Edinburgh office.

MARRIED MPs

Jennie and her husband Aneurin Bevin were the first British couple who were both MPs. Aneurin was the Minister of Health and Housing who led the creation of the National Health Service.

WHAT IS THE OPEN UNIVERSITY?

The Open University is different to other universities because it was founded to give people a second chance at doing further study. When it began, lots of its students were older because they had started working straight after leaving school.

Students at the Open University learn in their own time – often fitting their studies around their jobs – and wherever they already live. At first, television and radio were used for teaching, but now the work is done online with the support of tutors and lecturers.

KAYLEIGH HAGGO

Para Athlete

Born Irvine, Ayrshire, 1999

When Kayleigh watched her friends at primary school in Prestwick, Ayrshire, doing PE, she felt it was unfair that she could not join in. She has a condition called cerebral palsy, which affects her balance and movement. Her teachers did not know how to include her in sport and games, so instead they asked her to keep score from the sidelines.

Kayleigh remembers, "It was frustrating because I was a daredevil and I wanted to try everything. I was independent and didn't let my disability get to me even when I was younger. Whatever my peers were doing, I wanted to do it too."

"Whatever my peers were doing, I wanted to do it too."

Life changed for Kayleigh when she was 12 and her mum spotted a local 'come and try' event. Kayleigh had a shot at a sport called frame running – and loved it! She raced on a special three-wheeled bike that supported her upper body while her feet propelled her around the track.

Kayleigh says, "I'd never been able to run before, so it gave me such a sense of freedom! I didn't need anyone with me to make sure I wasn't going to fall; I could go around the track myself."

"It can be so easy to include everyone, it doesn't need to be complicated. Everyone deserves the chance to be involved in sport."

Frame running wasn't the only sport Kayleigh discovered she was good at. When she was a teenager, she spent four years swimming competitively. But in 2017, frame running became a World Para Athletics event and was included in the World Championships. Kayleigh gave up swimming and began frame running again. She trained for hours every day and dominated the sport.

Her most memorable sporting moment was winning her first gold medal for Great Britain in the 100m at the World Championships in Dubai in 2019. She remembers, "When I crossed the line, I burst into tears. I'd been training so hard and it was very emotional."

By the summer of 2021, she held the world records in the 100m, 200m, 400m, 800m, 1500m and 5,000m. She also became a world record holder in a different race classification, the T72 100m, in April 2023.

Kayleigh works to support herself, because frame running is not currently a Paralympic event so she doesn't receive funding to cover her training. But she is confident that frame running will one day be included. She says, "If it happened, I would hopefully receive funding to become a full-time athlete, which makes a huge difference to training. Competing in the Paralympics would be a dream come true."

GOOD NEIGHBOURS

During the coronavirus pandemic in 2020, Kayleigh had trouble getting hold of new gym equipment, but neighbours rallied around after she asked for help on social media. She says, "Soon I had everything I was looking for and more!" Kayleigh vowed to dedicate her next medal to the community.

Despite her success, Kayleigh has never forgotten that feeling of sitting on the sidelines. She came up with the idea for Inspire, her disability sports inclusion project, while studying for her degree in sports studies from the University of the West of Scotland. "We support coaches, volunteers and teachers to make sure everyone is included," Kayleigh explains. "I'm passionate about helping others." She also teaches courses and workshops for an organisation called Scottish Disability Sport.

Kayleigh believes, "Anything is possible if you put your mind to it. There may be barriers in the way, but think about what you can achieve by overcoming them."

DISCOVERING BOCCIA

In 2022, Kayleigh took up boccia, a sport designed for athletes with disabilities. Competitors throw, kick or use a ramp to propel a ball onto the court to get closest to a 'jack' ball. She was selected for her first international competition after playing for only four months, and won two out of three games.

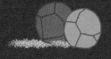

JANE HAINING

Missionary

Born Dunscore, Dumfriesshire, 1897

Jane grew up on a farm with her five sisters and father. Her mother died when she was just five, so the family looked after each other, finding comfort in their strong Christian faith.

At her village school, Jane excelled and was offered a scholarship to secondary school. After leaving Dumfries Academy as the dux (top of her year), Jane moved to Paisley to work as a clerk. Her faith was very important to her, and Jane attended church and taught Sunday School in nearby Glasgow. At a church meeting she learned about missionary work, which means telling people who are not Christian about Christianity. In 1932, Jane moved to Budapest, Hungary, to teach at the Scottish Jewish Mission School, run by the Church of Scotland.

The school had nearly 400 pupils, most of whom were Jewish. Of those, 30 to 40 were boarders, which meant they lived in the school. Jane was responsible for the girls who boarded and loved them all.

LEARNING THE LANGUAGE

Jane learned Hungarian, and taught in both English and Hungarian.

It was a terrible time for Jewish people. Adolf Hitler and the Nazis in Germany were attacking their homes, shops and synagogues.

Jewish people were prevented from practising professions like law, medicine and teaching, and forced to wear yellow Stars of David so they could be easily identified. Families were moved to crowded, dirty areas called ghettos, and Jewish children were not allowed to go to school. The Hungarian government followed the Nazis' example.

Yet Jane welcomed Jewish children even when other schools refused to teach them. She often reassured her girls, "You are loved and appreciated." Annette Lantos, one of Jane's pupils, remembers, "We all loved it there. It was like an island of tolerance among all the evil."

> **Jane's church told her to return to Scotland, but she refused to leave her girls.**

When the Second World War broke out, it became dangerous for Jane to remain in Budapest. Jane's church told her to return to Scotland, but she refused to leave her girls. Early every morning she went out to find them food, and she cut up her leather suitcase to mend their shoes.

In spring 1944, Germany invaded Hungary and the Gestapo arrested Jane, accusing her of being a spy. Fortunately

MEMENTOES OF JANE

In 2016, Jane's will, radio, typewriter, coat, photographs and watches were discovered in the Church of Scotland's World Mission Council in Edinburgh. They are now in the National Library of Scotland.

the girls, including Annette, escaped. But Jane was sent to Auschwitz, a concentration camp in Poland. She died two months later.

Her girls have never forgotten her. Annette says, "She exuded happiness, which was so unusual in those days. She shielded us and gave us a haven in the midst of all the hatred."

TRIBUTES TO COURAGE

Jane was recognised in 1997 as Righteous Among the Nations at Yad Vashem, the World Holocaust Remembrance Centre in Jerusalem, which commemorates non-Jews who took great risks to save Jews during the Holocaust. She is the only Scottish woman to receive this honour.

There are simple tributes to Jane's bravery in Scotland and Hungary. A cairn in Dunscore is dedicated to her, as is a stained-glass window in Queen's Park Govanhill Parish Church in Glasgow, where she used to worship. In 2010, the Hungarian government named a street running beside the River Danube in Budapest after her: Jane Haining Rakpart.

IONA FYFE
Singer-songwriter, Musician and Scots-language Activist
Born Aberdeen, 1998

Iona was very young when her parents split up, so for a while she and her mum lived with her gran. "We moved in with my nannie, and it was amazing having three generations under one roof," she says. At home, the family spoke Scots.

Soon after Iona and her mum moved to a council house in Huntly, Aberdeenshire, Iona started tinkling on her uncle's piano, which sparked a passion for music. She began piano lessons with a neighbour when she was six. "We were living in poverty, but Mum scrabbled together the money for tuition. I didn't go out to play that much because I was always practising. I loved it!" she says.

Iona and her friends spoke Scots in the school playground, and she also learned poetry in Doric. Her friends sometimes struggled to understand her passion for traditional music, but nevertheless Iona took part in competitions and joined in with trad singers in folk club 'singarounds'.

INSPIRATIONAL MUM

Iona's mum, Angela, was a huge influence. Iona says: "My mum had to keep a roof over my head. She was really strong. She's an amazing public speaker and I think I get my love of performing from her."

"Don't compare yourself with other people. Be proud of your achievements, be proud of who you are and where you come from."

As Iona's confidence grew, she performed bothy ballads: songs that had been sung on Aberdeenshire farms in local dialect for generations. At 16, she moved to Glasgow to study traditional music at the Royal Conservatoire of Scotland. Throughout her studies, she was also recording folk albums, winning awards and performing around the world.

HEALTH AND WELL-BEING

Iona has fibromyalgia, a condition that causes pain all over the body. She says, "Lady Gaga has it and raised awareness. It's really important that people realise that they can achieve things even when managing debilitating conditions."

Scots language is at the heart of Iona's music, and she also helped to found Oor Vyce, a campaign group dedicated to securing official recognition of the Scots language. They have lobbied 35 MSPs to sign a Scots Pledge to protect, fund and promote the language. In the 2011 census, 1.5 million people in Scotland spoke Scots.

MAKING HISTORY

Iona won the Scots Singer of the Year at the MG Alba Scots Trad Music Awards in 2018, and Scots Speaker of the Year in 2019. She made history by becoming the first singer to win Scots Musician of the Year in 2020.

IONA FYFE

Iona also successfully challenged Spotify to add Scots to its list of languages. She had tried to list her version of 'In The Bleak Midwinter' as Scots, but there was no option available for the language. "Every other minority language was there, like Manx, Cornish and Gaelic," she explains. "I wrote an open letter to Spotify and started tweeting them every day. There was so much red tape, but three months later they recognised Scots as a language!"

From singing to activism, Iona has made a huge contribution to traditional music and championing Scots.

> **"I wrote an open letter to Spotify... Three months later they recognised Scots as a language!"**

MIXING POLITICS AND MUSIC

Iona has a keen interest in politics and is a strong supporter of Scottish independence. She is a regional member of the Musicians' Union Scotland and Northern Ireland branch, and has spoken out about sexual harassment within the music industry, the effect of Brexit on live performers, and fair pay for musicians. In 2022 she won the Scottish Trades Union Congress Equality Award. She says, "By working with the Musicians' Union, I feel like I've been able to do politics and music."

NOSHEENA MOBARIK

Entrepreneur, Politician and Campaigner

Born Mian Channu, Pakistan, 1957

Nosheena was a little girl who loved talking, but when she moved from Pakistan to Scotland aged six, it became harder because she did not speak English. Yet soon she was fluent in her new language and settling into life in Glasgow. She says, "It was daunting being taken away from my childhood home, but I gradually started to fit in."

BALANCING STUDY AND MOTHERHOOD

When Nosheena's children were little, she went to university to study English literature and history. She says, "Going to university and juggling the children was one of the hardest things. I really had to take a deep breath and go for it."

When she was 19, Nosheena married her husband, Iqbal, and they had two children. She had a keen business brain and Iqbal had worked in his family's business while studying for a computing degree. Thinking they could work well together, they set up a business called M Computer Technologies. Their company was successful, and Nosheena realised she was

now in a position to help many other small family businesses. She got to know them and involved them in the wider business community.

Nosheena also created better connections between businesses in Scotland and Pakistan. In 2001 she was elected to the council of CBI (Confederation of British Industry) Scotland, an important business organisation. She remembers, "That first meeting I went to was so daunting, because I didn't know anyone and it was mostly men in the room. But I forced myself to go back and to get out of my comfort zone." Nosheena's efforts paid off: in 2011, she became CBI Scotland's chair.

Nosheena entered the House of Lords as life peer Baroness Mobarik.

Nosheena pushed herself even further when she became involved in politics. In 2014, a referendum asked Scotland's people whether it should remain part of the UK or become independent. Nosheena campaigned to remain and joined the Conservative Party. Later that year, she entered the House of Lords as life peer Baroness Mobarik. She also served in the European Parliament.

SPEAKING OUT

Nosheena's first speech (called a 'maiden speech') in the House of Lords was on modern slavery. This is when people are forced to work in terrible conditions without pay. It can happen to people who live in the UK or who have been brought here ('trafficked') from other countries. She described it as "one of the humanitarian catastrophes of our age".

NOSHEENA MOBARIK

When Nosheena was a little girl in a new country, she could never have guessed her love of connecting with people would lead to her becoming a successful businesswoman and a UK and European parliamentarian.

She says, "I've always been inquisitive and had a desire to learn, but I've also wanted to help people and do the right thing. I love being part of the scene and getting involved!"

HUMAN RIGHTS CAMPAIGNER

Charity work and promoting human rights are important to Nosheena. She was a co-founder of the Save the Bosnian People campaign in 1995, which raised money and organised humanitarian aid after war broke out in Yugoslavia.

Nosheena organised a multi-faith prayer vigil in Glasgow's City Chambers and says, "Leaders from different churches, mosques, temples, and synagogues were there. Between the different religions, there was warmth and kindness. As I've gone through life, I've realised my talent lies in bringing people together."

JESSIE VALENTINE

Golfer

Born Perth, 1915

Jessie grew up in Perth with her parents and her big sister. Her real name was Janet, but she was always called 'Wee Jessie'.

In 1920, Jessie's dad became the professional golfer attached to Braemar Golf Club, and took his five-year-old daughter to work with him. Even then Jessie's golf swing was practically perfect, and she spent hours practising with a club that was cut down to size for her.

Jessie gradually built up a selection of clubs: when she was twelve she had seven, and finally had a full set by the time she was seventeen, in 1932. That year she reached the semi-final of the British Girls Championship, and the following year she actually won. In 1934, she was selected to play for Scotland in the Home Internationals at famous golf club Royal Porthcawl, in Wales.

THE WRONG CLUB

Jessie was left-handed but played golf right-handed. This was perhaps because there were no left-handed girls' clubs in 1920.

Jessie was excited when she was invited to tour Australia and New Zealand in 1935 by the Ladies' Golf Union. She was nineteen and would be away from home for nearly five months. Jessie's dad was very proud that she had been

"Keep on trying with practice, practice, and more practice – by doing so, success will come your way."

selected and supported her decision to go. After a month-long journey on the liner RMS *Strathaird*, Jessie docked at Fremantle, Western Australia, for an amazing golfing adventure. She played in all the major cities of Australia and New Zealand.

ROUGH TIMES FOR FEMALE GOLFERS

Golf began in Scotland and has been played here since the 1450s. The first women's competition was played at Musselburgh Links in East Lothian in 1811, with a trophy and three blue silk hankies presented to the winner.

Women have faced discrimination in the sport and were banned from playing at some clubs, including in Scotland. In 2014, 260 years after it opened, the Royal and Ancient Golf Club of St Andrews finally voted to let female members join. And in 2017, after the course was stripped of its Open Championship host status, the Honourable Company of Edinburgh Golfers overturned the 228-year-long men-only rule at Muirfield.

Back in Scotland, Jessie won the 1937 British Ladies' Open at Turnberry, Ayrshire, and later that year was the World's No. 1 Lady Golfer, the equivalent of today's Women's World Golf Rankings. She would likely have won even more titles if it had not been for the outbreak of the Second World War in 1939. Jessie became an ambulance driver and had little opportunity to play. Her fiancé, George Valentine, was captured and held as a prisoner of war in Germany. But he survived, and the couple married after the war.

Up to this point in her career, Jessie was known as Jessie Anderson, but she was determined to have her married name engraved on a trophy. After turning her attention back to golf she was thrilled to achieve her aim by winning the British Ladies' Open again in 1955 and 1958.

Jessie might have been humble about her career, saying, "I visited many lands, met many people and achieved a few things," but there is no doubting her success. She dominated British golf for two decades and played the game well into her eighties. She became the first woman to receive an MBE for services to golf, and the name Wee Jessie became famous all over the world.

Jessie dominated British golf for two decades and played the game well into her eighties.

A LONG SHOT

In the 1936 Curtis Cup, Jessie holed a huge 6.5m putt under tremendous pressure on the eighteenth green to earn a draw for the British team against the United States.

LIFE AFTER GOLF

After Jessie stopped playing competitively, she designed clubs with Dunlop, and in 1967 she wrote a book called *Better Golf Definitely* to help golfers improve their game.

LAURA YOUNG
(LESS-WASTE LAURA)
Climate Activist
Born Rutherglen, Glasgow, 1996

Laura grew up close to the countryside in the southside of Glasgow with her parents and big brother. She loved going to the park and climbing hills. "I remember thinking and caring about the natural world," she says. "Recycling was always a part of my life even when I was young."

When Laura got older, she channelled her love of nature into studying geography, environmental science and, later, environmental protection. As she studied, public awareness of green issues increased hugely. Laura realised people were ready for change. She wondered whether she could show how every person can make a difference.

"Young people's voices have been heard in marches, in school strikes – they are the power behind change."

On New Year's Day in 2018, she made a start, saying: "I decided to reduce my waste. It was as simple as that." She set up a profile called @LessWasteLaura on social media, alongside a website and blog. "People were asking me for tips," she says. "I wanted to share my journey as well as knowledge about the planet, climate change and plastics."

"Don't ever be embarrassed about your passion or your hobby. Just go for it and have fun."

Soon, Laura was talking about how to help the environment to media organisations like Sky, STV and the BBC, and she gave a TED Talk in 2019 about not using plastic. She says, "People speaking about environmental issues aren't often young, Scottish females, so I can bring a different voice and perspective."

Alongside her voluntary activism, Laura worked at the international Christian development charity Tearfund, leading their Let's Change the Climate programme for churches across the UK. She also moderated a meeting between First Minister Nicola Sturgeon and faith leaders from five different countries at COP26, the United Nations climate change conference in Glasgow in 2021. She explains, "This meeting led to Scotland becoming the first developed nation to pledge money for loss and damage other countries have endured due to climate change."

FAITH IN ACTION

Laura's Christian faith motivates her environmentalism. She says, "I believe this world was created for us and it's our responsibility to look after it, but I'm also passionate about looking after people. People are impacted by climate change."

Laura believes young people are crucial in fighting climate change, saying, "We know what the problem is and we know what the solution is: we need renewable energy and less waste. But we need to move quicker. Young people's voices have been heard in marches, in school strikes – they are the power behind change."

WHAT IS CLIMATE CHANGE?

Climate change refers to shifts in weather patterns over a long period of time, such as different levels of rainfall and higher or lower temperatures. Our climate has constantly evolved, but it has been happening much more quickly over the last 50 to 100 years because of human activity. Using fossil fuels to power transport and industry emits gases that get trapped in the Earth's atmosphere and heat up the planet, melting polar ice caps and making sea levels rise. These changes affect everything and everyone on Earth.

SMALL CHANGES, BIG EFFECTS

Laura wants us all to understand how small changes we make can have big effects on other people we never see or know. She asks: "How can I love my neighbour in Uganda or Mexico who is facing climate change?" And she answers: "I can buy second-hand clothes, I can recycle, and I can walk to the shop instead of driving."

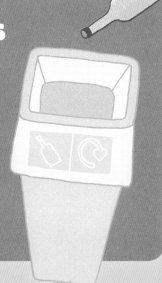

⭐ MY SPECTACULAR SCOTTISH WOMAN

Do you know someone who should be in this book? Maybe she's somebody famous who you admire, or maybe she's someone who is close to you. Create your own profile of a woman who inspires you.

WHAT IS YOUR SPECTACULAR WOMAN'S NAME?

WHAT DOES SHE DO?

WHERE AND WHEN WAS SHE BORN?

TELL HER SPECTACULAR STORY.

WRITE DOWN ONE OF HER SAYINGS.

"

"

DRAW HER PORTRAIT.

GLOSSARY

Apprenticeship: time spent working for an employer to learn the skills needed for a particular job.

Belt: 'getting the belt' was a type of physical punishment given out in schools. Teachers were allowed to strike pupils' hands with a leather belt. It was made illegal in the Education (No. 2) Act 1986.

Brexit: a combination of the words 'Britain' and 'exit', Brexit is the name given to the UK's departure from the European Union.

Campaign for Nuclear Disarmament (CND): a group that argues against having or using nuclear weapons.

Cerebral palsy: loss of control of movement in the arms and legs caused by damage to the brain or to brain development, usually before, during or just after birth.

Chair: the person in charge of the smooth running of a meeting or organisation.

Chronic fatigue syndrome: a long-term medical condition. The main symptoms are pain and extreme lack of energy that doesn't shift with ordinary rest.

Coming out: a phrase used to describe telling people about your sexual or romantic orientation, or your gender identity.

Communist Party: a political party that supports Communism, which is a way of organising society so that all the property and resources are owned by the government and shared out among the people.

COP26: COP stands for 'Conference of the Parties' and is the name given to the United Nations' climate change conferences. COP26 was the 26th conference, held in Glasgow in 2021.

COVID-19: a disease caused by a coronavirus. It was first identified in 2019 and infection spread to become a global pandemic in 2020.

Croft: a small piece of land on which a household lives and farms. Crofting is a way of organising land that has been an important part of life in the Scottish Highlands and Islands for the last 150 years, and that builds on earlier Gaelic traditions.

Discrimination: treating one person worse than another, or giving them fewer opportunities, due to their age, disability, gender, race, religion, sex or sexuality.

Doric: the Scots language as spoken in the north-east of Scotland.

Dunblane massacre: the deadliest mass shooting in British history, which took place in 1996 when a gunman killed 16 children and their teacher at Dunblane Primary School in central Scotland, and then shot himself. The massacre led to new laws restricting guns, and many safety measures at schools in Scotland.

Gaelic-medium education: a Scottish education system that teaches children primarily in the Gaelic language.

Gestapo: Nazi Germany's political police force.

Highland Clearances: in the late 1700s and 1800s, lairds in the Highlands removed people by force from land they had lived on all their lives so that the land would make more money, for example by being used to graze sheep. The Clearances led to desperate poverty and many people left Scotland and emigrated to other countries.

HIV and AIDS: HIV (human immunodeficiency virus) is the virus that can cause AIDS (acquired immune deficiency syndrome), a serious illness that affects the body's ability to fight infection.

Holocaust: the systematic killing of millions of Jewish people by the Nazis during the Second World War.

House of Commons: the part of the UK Parliament whose members (called 'members of parliament' or 'MPs') are elected by the public. The House of Commons proposes and debates new laws.

House of Lords: the part of the UK Parliament whose members (called 'peers') inherit their place, or gain it as part of another role (for example, in the church), or are chosen by the leaders of political parties.

Jacobite: supporters of the Stuart line of kings, especially the deposed King James II (1633–1701) and, later, his grandson, Charles Stuart (Bonnie Prince Charlie) (1720–1788), as opposed to the Protestant Hanoverian kings. The word Jacobite comes from 'Jacobus', which is Latin for James.

Kurdish people: an ethnic group native to Kurdistan, an area of western Asia that spans parts of Turkey, Iran, Iraq and Syria.

Life peer: a member of the House of Lords who has been given the title of 'peer' and the right to sit in the House of Lords for their lifetime. Unlike hereditary peers, life peers cannot pass their title to their children or grandchildren.

Lockerbie bombing: Pan Am Flight 103 exploded over the town of Lockerbie in south-west Scotland on 21 December 1988, after a bomb was detonated on board. All 259 passengers were killed along with 11 people in Lockerbie.

Prisoner of war: someone captured by the opposing side during a war.

Referendum: a vote that takes place when a government asks the people to decide a particular political question, such as whether Scotland should be part of the United Kingdom.

Slum: a poor area of a city where the housing and facilities are in very bad condition.

Socialism: a way of organising society to share resources and wealth more equally.

Suffrage: the right to vote in political elections.

Suffragists: women in the late nineteenth and early twentieth centuries who campaigned for women to have the right to vote and to participate in elections.

Suffragists campaigned peacefully, using persuasion. The suffragettes used direct action – such as disrupting meetings or events, smashing windows and setting fire to postboxes – to express their anger that women had to obey laws but could not vote for the politicians who made them.

Traveller community: specific groups of people with a nomadic tradition, which means they move from place to place rather than having a fixed home. While the Traveller community has a long history in Scotland and a rich culture of story and song, it has often experienced discrimination.

Working class: people whose jobs usually involve physical work. These jobs are usually paid less than jobs that require more educational qualifications. Historically, working-class people did not have political power as individuals, so they often banded together to gain greater say over the conditions of their own lives.

LOUISE BAILLIE'S ACKNOWLEDGEMENTS

To Iris and Megan, I'm so proud of you both. Thanks to Craig for the encouragement, and the endless cups of coffee. Love you all.

Thanks to my mum, Rosemary, and my dad, Rodger, for giving me the joy of reading and writing, and to my whole family for their love and support.

Lots of love to all my spectacular friends, for being with me every step of the way, particularly when I couldn't walk. Alyson, Abi, and Rona thanks for everything, and Lindsey, this might not have happened without you. I'm so grateful for all my amazing friends.

LOUISE BAILLIE was a journalist for almost 20 years and loved to work on both news stories and in-depth features. She was inspired to write *Spectacular Scottish Women* because she wanted to encourage her daughters' energy and ambition, and give them stories of achievement that they could relate to.

Louise called on her journalistic background while conducting the interviews and research that led to these incredible true stories. Louise now works in communications at a children's rights organisation.

She loves running, playing tennis (badly) and football. Louise lives in Glasgow with her husband, two daughters, and their black Labrador Luna.

 is an illustrator and teacher at Edinburgh College of Art. Her books include *Fierce, Fearless and Free* (traditional tales starring amazing women and girls), picture book *Snooze* and a collection of colouring books for adults.

Eilidh drew the illustrations for *Spectacular Scottish Women* using a mixture of pencils, fineliner pens, and messy ink. She did a lot of research to help her capture the personality of each woman, and particularly loved creating the portrait of one of her heroes, artist Joan Eardley. She can't wait to share this book with her daughter when she's old enough.

Eilidh loves walking, swimming and being in the outdoors. She lives near Edinburgh with her family and Maggie the Border Collie.

DISCOVER SCOTLAND...
SPECTACULAR STORIES

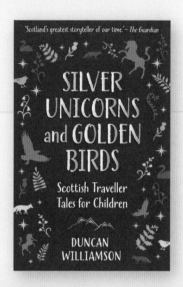

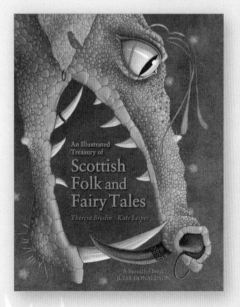

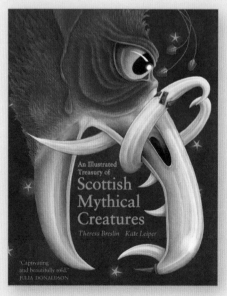

DiscoverKelpies.co.uk

TRADITIONAL SCOTTISH TALES

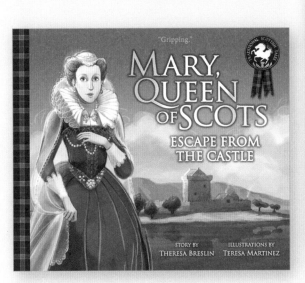

"Gripping."

MARY, QUEEN OF SCOTS
ESCAPE FROM THE CASTLE

STORY BY
Theresa Breslin

ILLUSTRATIONS BY
Teresa Martinez

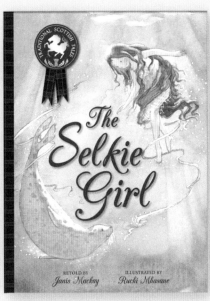

The Selkie Girl

RETOLD BY
Janis Mackay

ILLUSTRATED BY
Ruchi Mhasane

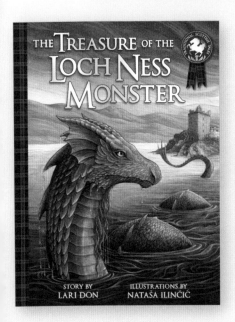

THE TREASURE OF THE LOCH NESS MONSTER

STORY BY
LARI DON

ILLUSTRATIONS BY
NATAŠA ILINCIC

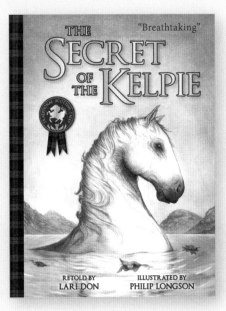

"Breathtaking"

THE SECRET OF THE KELPIE

RETOLD BY
LARI DON

ILLUSTRATED BY
PHILIP LONGSON

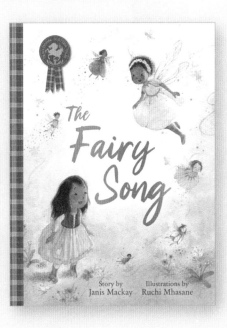

The Fairy Song

Story by
Janis Mackay

Illustrations by
Ruchi Mhasane

DiscoverKelpies.co.uk

AMAZING ATLASES

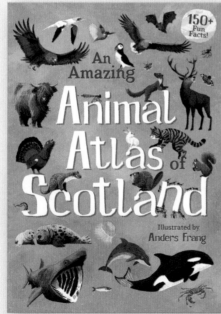

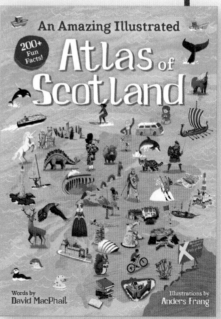

DiscoverKelpies.co.uk